A SNOWY WHITE CHRISTMAS

A Contemporary Sweet Romance Novella

JOSIE RIVIERA

This book is dedicated to all my wonderful readers who have supported me every inch of the way.

THANK YOU!

INTRODUCTION

To keep up on newly released ebooks, paperbacks, Large Print Paperbacks, audiobooks, as well as exclusive sales, sign up for Josie's Newsletter today.

As a thank you, I'll send you a Free PDF ... The Beauty Of ...

Josie's Newsletter

Did you know that according to a Yale University study, people who read books live longer?

A Snowy White Christmas

PRAISE AND AWARDS

USA TODAY bestselling author

ACKNOWLEDGEMENTS

To my patient husband, Dave, and our three wonderful children.

CHAPTER ONE

Sometimes Margaret Snow's guilt would go away for a few minutes. But it always returned. Insistent. Dull. Intense.

She was a terrible mother. Check.

She'd never amount to anything. Check.

She only thought about herself. Check.

These negative thoughts chattered incessantly, tucked ever so slightly behind everyday activities. Like uncaged wild animals waiting to pounce at the first opportunity.

She glanced out her office window. Despite the wind and ice, city workers were adding cheery red bells and silver holiday trimmings to the streetlights. It didn't help. November in upstate New York promised gray skies, bitter sleet, and not an ounce of cheeriness until spring. Today was no exception.

What was the weather like in California? She checked the weather app on her phone. As expected, sunny skies in Los Angeles were predicted throughout the Thanksgiving holiday.

"Unbelievable," she whispered. "How could two places be so different?"

And why was she stuck in the lesser desirable of the two?

It was her own fault. She'd forgotten her lines during her last audition because she'd been preoccupied with her daughter's insistent cough that had lingered for weeks. But her agent, Sid, and the casting director hadn't been interested in excuses, and they just dismissed her as a wannabe actress who didn't take the acting profession seriously.

"Stick to modeling," they'd said.

She sighed. She'd been back in her depressing hometown only three weeks and already felt limp and exhausted.

But her daughter Amelie seemed content, and only Amelie mattered. Margaret grinned, remembering the impish smile Amelie would flash whenever she had rolled round and round on their favorite California beach. She'd emerge covered in sand, her small eyeglasses placed carefully on a nearby towel. Her incessant coughing spells would follow, but the physician assistant she saw assured Margaret this was normal in a frail child, and as long as Amelie didn't develop a fever, there was no need for concern.

"See? I'm fine, Mom," Amelie would say, giggling while demonstrating a perfect cartwheel in the sand. "Now let's go for peppermint ice cream."

Margaret's heart did a funny little turn. Amelie was so much like her father. A perfectionist and a planner. And that was why she'd ensured that Amelie would never know him.

Grumpy, her African grey parrot hanging upside down from the top of its cage, chirped an out-of-tune melody.

"Talk. Say something," she said, knowing he couldn't hear her.

He stared back and shook his head.

She sipped her cup of cold black coffee and shuffled through the stack of blank applications on her desk. The famous actress she'd hoped to become was now relegated to this, a talent agent looking for talent in a town that had none.

So demeaning, but at least she was able to provide for her daughter. She sighed, louder this time, twisted the wadded-up handkerchief on her lap and dabbed at her eyes.

A familiar Christmas carol played faintly on the radio, an instrumental arrangement of "Jingle Bells." Shouldn't there be a law prohibiting the playing of Christmas music before Thanksgiving? She clicked it off and gazed absently at the cornucopia wreath tacked lopsided on her office door. Her office was a mess, with boxes piled in a far corner, but she'd only been in Owanda a few weeks and hadn't had time to unpack.

A loud knock brought her attention to the present. Lucy, Margaret's best friend since childhood, opened the door. "Are you busy? You are, right?" She blinked twice, the signal they'd devised years ago for impending disaster.

"Should I be?" Margaret stuffed the handkerchief into her skirt pocket and set the coffee cup on her desk. Formalities weren't observed in upstate New York. One simply rapped on the door and barged in because everyone was considered family. But the only family she'd known lived in a fairy tale. No mother had ever bounced her on her knees or sung lullabies at night. Her mother had been too busy hiding from her drunken, violent husband.

"One of your elves is here for his interview." Lucy actually said this with a straight face. Her blonde hair was styled into an angled bob, soft wisps cascading around her broad cheekbones. She never left the house unless she looked picture-perfect, even if she was only heading to the grocery store. Hollywood had changed her. It had changed them both.

"I tried to stop him, but he knows us too well." Lucy stepped closer and cupped her hands around Margaret's ear. "And take my word, he really knows *you*."

Sure he did. Margaret felt the scowl settle on her forehead. She'd been a swimsuit model, and men had excellent memories when it came to bikinis and the women who filled them. She'd never modeled topless—never. But skimpy? Well ... yes, if it paid the bills and Amelie's tuition. And this elf could request her autograph with a gold pen and silver paper, but he'd be leaving her office empty-handed.

Lucy shook her head. "He was always so demanding."

He was always ...

"Send him in," Margaret replied. She'd dealt with pushy fans before. He could take his autograph book and—

But he'd already barged into her office, all six feet of charm. He was, after all, from upstate New York. See above if you forgot.

With a wave as if she were leaving for a trip abroad, Lucy said, "I'm in my office if you need me." She retreated into the hallway and closed the door.

"My lovely princess," he was saying, "you're as beautiful as ever." He glanced at the parrot. "And I see some things never change. Your house always resembled a pet hotel."

She gaped, stunned by the deep voice and all-too-familiar endearment.

She caught her reflection in the mirror on the opposite wall. "Mirror, mirror, who's the fairest?" he'd always teased. She wasn't beautiful, but her cheekbones were high and her skin smooth and clear. The rest of her had been gangly arms and legs and too-dark eyebrows.

Was she sitting or standing? All the poise and modeling classes were forgotten in the space of a second. Fernando. Fernando. Fernando. It couldn't be, not after all these years. She drew in a breath and held it.

He brushed a hand through his dark hair, dampened from the icy weather. "I heard you were back in town."

She swallowed. How did a man look so put together in this type of weather? Her voice returned and matched her shaking body. "You live in Owanda?"

"I thought I did, although you're making me question it."
He looked around, a slight smile gracing his mouth.
"Remember we lived two blocks from each other?"

Except she'd lived in the double-wide trailer at the edge of
a trailer park and he'd lived in a cozy bungalow with white
shingles and a red front door. She looked off for a moment,
needing to focus on something else, anything else. Grumpy
appeared to be sleeping.

"How could I ever forget?" she asked.

Fleeting hurt dimmed his gaze, but the smile remained.
"You forgot quickly, actually." He took a step forward, seemed
to think better of getting closer, and halted. "I've missed
you." He glanced at the parrot. "Don't tell me, let me guess.
He's blind."

"Deaf."

"Does he talk?"

"No, but sometimes he sings off-key." She looked pointedly toward the street. "Probably because he's speechless at
the terrible weather."

Fernando laughed. "It's not so bad here. Summers are very
pleasant."

It took everything in her to remain calm and silent. He
was digging in for more conversation, offering small talk
before he began his interrogation.

"I brought you a gift." He retrieved a small box, wrapped
in gold foil paper with a silver bow, from beneath his wool
coat and held it out to her. "Welcome home."

"Thank you, Fernando, but this isn't home." There. She
was able to say his name aloud.

When they'd been together, he'd always surprised her with
little wrapped gifts—her favorite drugstore perfume, tech-
nical books about nursing injured animals, a small leather
journal for her notes. Inside the package he'd always write in

his bold, neat script: "To my snow white princess, all my love."

"And I can't accept any gifts," she added.

"Of course, you can." His dark brown eyes gleamed with a certainty that she would, indeed, accept it. He carried his belief confidently on his muscular shoulders that life around him went according to his plans. He hadn't changed.

"No, I can't." She pushed back her chair so quickly, it clattered to the floor. Gracefulness had never been her forte and, yes, she'd been sitting. Fortunately, the falling chair gave her something to do—scramble and bend to retrieve it, taking longer than necessary because frustration and memories collided. When she stood, she held the chair upright in front of her like a lion tamer. She'd read a magazine article that a lion tamer used the chair in the ring to confuse the lion, not as a form of defense. All she needed was a whip in the other hand, but the same article had assured that the tamer's whip was only for show. So she stood face to face with Fernando, holding a useless chair and a non-existent whip that wouldn't have helped anyway. Tanned and attractive, he watched her with desire in his gaze. He resembled a sexy magazine ad for a man who desperately needed a shave and didn't care.

He moved her small Christmas tree to the corner of her desk, then placed his gift on the opposite corner. "Please. I bought this especially for you many years ago."

"What are you doing in my office?" Not waiting for a reply, she turned and placed the chair behind her. Swiveling back, she smoothed her lemon-colored skirt and focused on the framed photo hanging on the opposite wall. In the photo she was arm in arm with a famous male actor, and they both held a glass of champagne. Her silk dress was low cut, inappropriately tight, and beyond short. What had they been toasting? She couldn't remember. Her hazel eyes in the photo stared back, glassy with too much drink. Her gaze darted to Fernando. His smile had changed, now slow and insolent as if he'd read her mind and agreed she'd been too provocatively dressed for a twenty-year-old girl. The gleam in his eyes was gone, and he'd reverted to his default setting of disapproval, one of his favorite settings. She'd never met his expectations of the cloyingly cute, content upstate New York girl.

"I thought you lived in Los Angeles," he said. "That swimsuit photo shoot you were in for the sports magazine was the main topic of conversation in this town for several weeks. You and that minuscule yellow bikini made the cover."

"I do. I did. What did you say you're doing here?" She braced both hands on the edge of her desk. Her palms were sweating. What was the advice when confronted with an uncomfortable situation? Stay calm and imagine the other person naked. Yikes! That didn't work as images of his naked, muscular body flooded her senses. She inhaled so loudly, the sound filled the stark room. As she fingered the wadded handkerchief in her skirt pocket, her gold bracelets jingled with a busy clink, reflecting her agitation. Lazy afternoons in his bed when they'd ducked out of high school early were forever seared into her brain. Years of therapy obviously hadn't helped. One minute with him and she reverted to a flustered schoolgirl.

An impish grin moved across his face.

"I'd heard you'd moved out of the area and worked in Florida for some real estate company," she said.

"Don't believe everything you hear. I'm back and forth." His gaze lingered on the top buttons of her blouse. "I'd read in one of the tabloids you were considered for a leading role in a Hollywood adventure film."

She stiffened. "Don't believe everything you read."

Rejection was part of the acting business. Her agent had explained that the role had ultimately been given to a younger upcoming actress who'd worked in classical theater. "Things will pick up in January," he'd assured her.

Fernando shook his head. "An adventure film doesn't seem suitable for an actress with your talent. You probably would've been running around scantily clothed while the action took place all around you." His tone held kindness and understanding. "Besides, the role was for a blonde, and you wouldn't want to change your hair color again. You're stunning when you're a brunette."

"Thanks. I'll be sure to pass your opinion on to my agent." She resisted the urge to touch her hair and shuffled the applications on her desk instead.

"Are you in Owanda for a couple of days visiting friends?"

Please be here for a short while. Like one day. In the meantime, she calculated how long it would take to pack her and Amelie's suitcases and leave town. Two days, maybe three. And how would Amelie adjust to the news? Today was her first day at a reputable public school for the deaf and things were settling into a new normal. Margaret squeezed her eyes shut for a moment. She needed this job to buy back her trailer. She needed a big break in Hollywood so that Amelie could return to her private school. She needed to get out of this decrepit town if Fernando was here.

His gaze had taken permanent residence on the low neckline of her green blouse. "No friends you'd know." He loosened the wool scarf around his neck and turned to the window, a look of feigned surprise on his face. "So you're gracing us with your famed presence because you'd prefer to interview elves rather than star in million-dollar movies or appear on the covers of magazines? Are the paparazzi camped outside? I don't remember seeing any."

"They couldn't work on their suntans in upstate New York."

"Are you visiting anyone special for Thanksgiving? Your parents passed away a few years ago."

Probing, as usual. Leave. Please leave. Don't ask any more questions.

She swallowed. "Yes, both my parents are gone." Always, the sorrow she should've felt wasn't there.

Sadness blurred his striking features and tiny lines creased his forehead. His face showed his thoughts like a road map, although the road map looked more mature and a tad worn. Perhaps he'd aged as much in six years as she had.

"I'm sorry for your loss," he was saying. "They weren't perfect, but I believe they loved you very much."

"They didn't, but thanks." Her throat ached at the recollection of the childhood whippings she'd endured at the hands of her father while her mother sat silent.

"You're still a woman of few words," he said.

"Who's interviewing whom?"

"Just like old times. I talked and you responded in monosyllables. I never knew what you were thinking."

She shifted. "Why are you here again?"

He unbuttoned his long gray wool coat. The sable-black scarf hung loosely around his neck. "Don't you know why?"

"No, I don't, but if this is a game and I'm supposed to guess, then I'll change the subject to the weather because I'm not good at guessing." She glanced at the clock. Still time to make an escape from his certain interrogation. "How's this? I haven't experienced a white Christmas in a long time."

"I only returned a few months ago, but I imagine the winters are as harsh as ever," he said.

"So you live in Florida? The weather is warm and sunny there."

"I didn't say for certain, but I appreciate you trying to check up on where I live." That seemed to please him, and a smile appeared. "You looked surprised when I walked in."

Surprised? Talk about understatements. An eye roll was in order, but he was watching too closely. She stood straighter. "You mean when you barged in. And yes, you were the last person I ever expected to see again."

"After high school graduation, there was nothing left for me, so I left the area," he said.

"You always said you liked this depressing, freezing town."

"Owanda is comfortable and familiar, but it wasn't the same without you."

Because you disappeared without a word. He didn't say it. He didn't have to. His road-map features showed anger, then hurt. Why couldn't he hide his emotions? All the men in Hollywood said one thing while meaning another. But they were actors and agents, and he was an open, honest canvas. Right and wrong. There was no gray area for him.

"You know I needed more than what Owanda offered," she said.

"Certainly more than I could ever offer."

The gentleness in his voice was unexpected, and the shock she'd felt when he entered was draining away to something else. He'd offered her caring and security. And love.

She suppressed a rush of sudden tears. "I've never been satisfied. I wanted more than a Saturday night at the local movie theater followed by a keg party."

"A woman as lovely as you wanted something better than a guy from a small town who spent his nights partying."

"You were popular. Hockey team, class president, you managed it all."

He smiled. "I was always true to you."

His smile was so genuine, she returned it. "I know you were."

They were allies for a moment. But if he suspected she was hiding anything, he'd board the truth train and never get off. She snapped her thoughts away from panic and inhaled a steadying breath. He'd never know. He'd never know.

He held up his hands, palms out, a gesture of understanding. "I'm not asking for an explanation for why you left. I've never analyzed people's motives nor judged them."

"You've always been the better person."

When you weren't drinking.

He dropped his hands. "So you decided to leave sunny Los Angeles to work for your former talent agency at the coldest time of the year and interview elves?"

"It's temporary. I'm between jobs and doing my agency a favor."

She was desperate.

"Plus," she continued, "this allows me an opportunity to spend the holidays in an authentic winter setting to research my next role as a snow princess in Alaska. Of course, the screenplay is only in the planning stages." She glanced at him, hoping he actually believed her story. He seemed relaxed, his expression suggesting interest. Perhaps she was a better actress than her agent thought.

He nodded. "The weather doesn't get any more wintry than upstate New York."

"For this current project, my agency has asked me to audition men four feet ten inches or shorter for jobs at the mall as Santa's helpers." She glanced at the neatly wrapped package on her desk. "If you're trying to bribe me with a gift to get a job ..." She gazed up at his tall, lean frame and gave a rueful laugh. "Sorry. You don't fit the role requirements."

His gaze locked with hers, a wry smile on his lips. "Actually, I'm here to represent my twin brother, Michael. If you recall, he's a dwarf."

She nodded slowly. "Of course. I'm sorry, I'd forgotten about him."

Years ago, she'd enjoyed weekly Sunday dinners at Fernando's home. Michael had worn a hearing aid because the bones in his ears were so small, but the Brandts' good-natured teasing and shouting made up for any hearing impediment. She'd learned sign language because of Michael. Ironic, as signing was one of the main forms of communication she used with Amelie. The remembrance of mouthwatering sausages, green vegetables, and sauerkraut simmering on the Brandt kitchen stove teased her nostrils. His mother was Spanish—hence Fernando's Spanish name—but had cooked German food to please her husband.

Margaret had sworn off German food after leaving Owanda because it brought back too many memories. His family had been so demonstrative, so caring, so unlike her own. Her mother had never cooked a hot meal. In fact, she'd never cooked any meal. And Margaret had had only two conversations with her father in her entire life. Both times he'd been sober. Two times, in eighteen years.

Fernando's mother had always sent Margaret home with leftovers in case there wasn't any food in her house. There never was.

She cleared her throat. "I didn't advertise for dwarfs."

"You advertised for elves, but dwarf is a politically correct term. Michael can be Sneezy today because he's coughing and having chest pain. However, I took him to our family physician, and he's fine." Fernando smiled. He had those crinkly laugh lines around his eyes she remembered so well. "Now you only need to find six more dwarfs. What were their names again?"

She held up a hand. "Thanks, I know the names of the seven dwarfs. And I'm looking for elves, not dwarfs marching off to a mine every morning."

"The dwarfs were searching for diamonds. Some were kept and some were discarded, but all diamonds are rare and precious." He gave her a long, appreciative look and then glanced at the applications on her desk. "The economy didn't recover here as well as it did in other parts of the country. Most people in our town will take any job available."

Our town. Owanda was his town but it certainly wasn't her town. She was a California girl now.

She offered him an application and pen. "I need to leave soon, so you can mail it back to the agency. The address is at the top."

"This won't take long." He grabbed the pen and pulled a chair up to the opposite side of her desk. He shrugged off his coat and scarf, slung both behind the chair, and sat. His absorption in the application gave her time to retuck her blouse into her skirt and quickly feel that all the buttons were securely fastened. She lifted her chin and offered an in-control smile just in case he looked up, hoping she gave the appearance of a self-confident movie star. If only she could wipe away the sweat gathering beneath her fringe of bangs without looking insecure.

She glanced at the clock. Two fifteen. Amelie was dismissed from school at three o'clock.

He pushed the application toward her, along with the business card he recovered from the pocket of his well-tailored gray suit. "I'll give you one of my cards."

"Thanks." She stuffed the card into the top drawer of her desk without looking at it, along with his gift.

He quirked a dark brow but said nothing.

She perused his neat handwriting on the application, instantly recognizable even after all these years. Her mother had forwarded his unopened letters to California. He'd written her love letters pleading with her to return. He'd admitted he had an addictive personality and vowed to give up drinking.

She never answered him. At eighteen years old and pregnant, the bright lights of Hollywood were a beacon for a wealthy new life she could achieve on her own merit. She was an independent woman who relied on no man.

She studied the application. "Your brother still lives at your old address?"

Fernando loosened his navy tie. "Yes."

"With your parents?"

"Sadly, my father passed away several years ago. Michael lives with my mother, although he had his own apartment for several years. Lately he's prone to seizures, and I insisted he no longer live alone. He's also recovering from a major operation."

"I'm sorry. I hope he's up to working."

Fernando's gaze drilled into hers with a silent plea. "Work is the best therapy for his recuperation, and it will take his mind off his ailments. Nothing like being an elf in the world of make-believe to forget all your cares."

A beat passed.

"Without dreams, life would be boring and empty," she said.

"Keep your head in the clouds if you want to, but your feet should be firmly on the ground." A deep smile emphasized his dimple. He hadn't outgrown the light sprinkling of freckles on his nose and cheeks. He'd been the best-looking guy in the senior class, rugged and lean, his T-shirt worn untucked. He'd offered her love, but now something else simmered beneath the surface, a resolve edged with tenacity.

He studied her face. "This is the point where you're supposed to press me for details about my life."

She offered him an indifferent shrug. He returned the shrug. A shrug contest. Who could act the most disinterested?

"All right, if you're not interested in me, let's talk about Michael." He leaned back in the chair and crossed his arms.

"Do you have any information regarding the job? That is, if you decide to hire him."

She grinned. "There's a shortage of elves in Owanda, so he's got the job. The local mall is setting up a Christmas display in its center court and needs several elves to assist Santa while the children wait in line to see him." She scanned the application. "You listed Michael's phone number and e-mail, so I'll contact him directly. The job will begin the day after Thanksgiving and end Christmas Eve. I hope he's prepared to work nights and weekends, because Christmas isn't all fun and games."

"Of course it is." His dark eyes were filled with warmth again. "I love Christmas."

Snowball fights in the Brandts' backyard. Multi-colored lights and silvery tinsel decorating the Christmas tree, the scent of fresh pine in their living room. The savory aromas of almond crescents and cinnamon stars wafting from the warm kitchen.

Her own childhood house with no Christmas tree, broken lights permanently strung along their front porch, and a drunken, drug-addicted father permanently strung out on the living room couch.

She chewed her bottom lip, a habit from childhood. Her voice softened. "Christmas isn't joyful for many people."

"You and I used to laugh together, sometimes over the silliest jokes. You loved holidays, especially Christmas."

"I'm an aspiring actress. Maybe I was pretending."

He shook his head. "I know you well. Very well. You weren't acting."

She waved a hand dismissively. He was watching her too closely. "Christmas is for children."

"Christmas is for everyone." His voice had a slight catch, but perhaps she imagined it. "Nothing is more precious than seeing a child's face on Christmas morning and the assurance everything's right in the world."

His words almost finished her. Tears sprang to her eyes. There wasn't room in the air for shiny expensive gifts and high expectations. The clock on the wall ticked the minutes, hours, days. Only forty days until Christmas. She'd never be able to stay in Owanda if he were here. She straightened her shoulders and met his probing stare, reminding herself she was not the destitute, dependent girl she'd once been.

CHAPTER TWO

Fernando was the one to break the stare. He glanced at his gold watch for the second time in five minutes. It must be fake, she thought. He could never afford anything so expensive.

"I'm late for a meeting, but can we get together while you're here?" he asked. "I'm certain my mother would want to see you for a chat. And our favorite pizzeria, Antonio's, is still in business. We can enjoy a pizza and grab a slice of ricotta cheesecake for dessert."

And there he went, planning her life right down to dessert.

She kept her expression nondescript. "I can't commit because of my schedule. I'm sure you understand."

The perfect vague excuse people used to get out of things they didn't want to do. People always prioritized what was important to them and what wasn't. In truth, she wasn't about to chat with his mother in her intimate kitchen about a Christmas sugar cookie recipe or how California weather differed from New York's. Not when there was a matter of far greater importance his mother knew nothing about.

"Of course," he said. "You're a successful model with a full agenda. You've gotten exactly what you've always wanted."

"There's nothing wrong with being financially independent."

He pointed to the photograph on the opposite wall. "Even if it means giving up your integrity? That's not the woman I knew." With a nod, he stood, pulled on his coat and scarf and strode to the office door.

Only he wasn't striding, he was limping and holding his side.

"Are you hurt?" she asked.

He turned. "Just a sprain. I was working on my car yesterday."

"You always said you weren't mechanical and didn't know the difference between a steering shaft and a steering wheel."

"People change." He looked at his watch again. Three times since he'd entered her office. And his cell phone kept buzzing. "Good-bye, Margaret. I hope your Christmas display is a success."

That was it? He wasn't going to press to see her again?

She gazed at him, this darkly attractive man who was looking more amused than disinterested, and stepped around her desk. "Fernando, wait."

She didn't want him to leave. She didn't want him to stay. A tenderness for him, a rush of longing, made her want to explain, if only she could. *I'm not rich any more. Your beautiful daughter looks like you. She has your eyes, your smile, and your kind heart.*

But she'd never tell him because he'd never allow them to leave if he knew the truth. So instead she said, "I'd enjoy seeing your mother again."

She mentally shrugged, telling herself he'd hound her until she consented anyway. Besides, she loved his mother's sugar cookies, as well as pizza and ricotta cheesecake from Antonio's.

"I invited you to spend a relaxing evening with me. It's not a jail sentence." He ran a finger along her chin. "So you can smile."

She obliged, hesitantly. "Sounds perfect. And I'm looking forward to seeing your brother again."

Something sad crossed Fernando's face, but was quickly replaced by his usual optimistic grin. His finger glided to her cheek. So light, so exquisite. So like him to roll kindness and encouragement into a caress.

"Michael faced some challenges this past year. He was on dialysis, but they found a kidney donor, and he's much better. This job will be good because he needs to know that he matters and is a useful working adult."

"Of course he matters. Michael was such a contented, carefree child."

"He's still mildly autistic."

"He was all the more loving because of his autism. I remember when I was at your house, he was obsessed with driving a cherry-red toy train across your mother's dining room table. She'd scold him, but everyone knew she didn't mind."

The laughter and joking had been nonstop at the Brandts'. Her eyes welled. Amelie had a loving family she'd never meet.

She reached to wipe a tear away, but Fernando was faster. He tipped up her chin. "These are happy memories."

She attempted a laugh. "I never used to cry, but now I get weepy all the time."

He grabbed her hand and held it. "Michael's red train sits safely on a shelf in his bedroom, although he doesn't play with toy trains anymore." One corner of his mouth twitched, and he looked suspiciously like he was laughing at her.

She'd been made fun of enough in her life. She shrugged off his hands.

He backed away. "You're a self-sufficient woman now. Forgive me for forgetting." The cell phone in his coat pocket buzzed again. He ignored it.

"I cried when I was younger," he said softly.

This was unexpected. She forced a quiet, disbelieving laugh.

"You called me a baby once," he said.

She shifted. She remembered but couldn't recall why she'd been so angry and had lashed out at him. "I'm sorry. I'll blame it on being young and ignorant. I now know there's nothing wrong with a man showing his emotions. It's a sign of strength, not weakness."

"I never cry anymore," he said. "I quickly learned crying doesn't change anything."

She wanted to run her hand reassuringly along the dark bristles on his strong, determined chin, but her arms felt too heavy, and she couldn't lift them. And the room was too hot. Maybe she was getting a fever. She needed some fresh air and glanced toward the window. No yellow ball of California sunshine shone back, only gray, gloomy skies. A worker bundled in a hooded, military-green parka was sweeping the sleet from the sidewalk.

The clock chimed two thirty.

"Perhaps," he said, "that's the reason why you decided not to date me." He grabbed the door handle and opened the door a crack. He hunched over but quickly straightened.

Margaret figured Lucy had her ear pressed to the door and was eavesdropping on the entire conversation and was surprised her friend didn't fall into the room.

"Don't assume you know everything about me," she said.

He stepped back toward her. She breathed in his familiar scent of the outdoors and cold air. No expensive men's cologne for him. "But I do know everything about you." His tone had changed, warmer now, sensual.

No, no. Not this. She moved away. "We never agreed about anything."

"We agreed about one thing," he said. "And beneath your stardom and expensive clothes, you're still the same passionate woman. Somewhere along the way you've lost sight of what's important. I understand."

"I have a therapist in Los Angeles. I don't need your advice."

He grabbed her shoulders and pulled her closer. His dark brown eyes reminded her of melted chocolate. "You'll find everything you're looking for right here."

She wasn't prepared for the tenderness in his voice. "Who am I, Dorothy from *The Wizard of Oz*?" She jerked away. "I'm not wearing ruby slippers and don't need a lecture. There's nothing in this depressing town for me."

He brushed his fingers along her cheek. "You used to enjoy when I held you. You said it was comforting." His glance slid to her lips.

She inhaled sharply. "Not every situation can be arranged by you because—"

"Of course it can." His arms locked around her, and his lips came down on hers in a long, demanding kiss. "So enchanting."

She leaned against him as he deepened the kiss. He'd been so good to her and they fit so well together. Her perfect match. Her soul mate. Her protector.

"My stunning princess," he whispered. "You're as beautiful as Snow White."

She twined her arms around his neck. She shouldn't. She did. She'd always loved when he'd called her Snow White because of her shiny ebony hair, chin length and parted in the middle and her contrasting pale skin. A thousand lifetimes ago. But life changes—one last time in his bed, an unplanned pregnancy, a resolve to pursue her dreams.

She drew a great gulp of air and dropped her hands. "I have to leave."

"So do I." Melted chocolate cooled, and he moved back a step. "When can I see you again?"

Never. Had she said the word aloud?

CHAPTER THREE

S he must have, considering how quickly his gaze turned cold.

She turned to the closet in the corner of her office, pulled on a royal-blue coat lined with a fleece collar, and tied a checkered scarf around her neck.

"Am I being dismissed?" he asked.

She slung her black leather tote over her shoulder. "You're not the only person with commitments."

Lucy chose that perfect moment to appear in the doorway. "Margaret, don't forget your three o'clock appointment."

"You're ever efficient, Lucy," he said. "Always hovering over Margaret like the older sister she never had."

"So glad to see you, Fernando." Lucy narrowed her eyes. Her bubble-gum pink lipstick had faded. "What are you doing here? I was told you'd left town years ago."

He turned up the collar of his coat, genuine puzzlement on his face. "And why would you have inquired about my whereabouts?"

"Lucy was looking up people from our high school yearbook in case anyone wanted to get together for a Christmas reunion,"

Margaret smoothly interjected. She certainly was honing her acting skills today. Her next audition was bound to be a success.

"Are you living in Owanda or just visiting?" Lucy asked him.

"That seems to be the question of the day, and I assure you I'm not peddling apples." He smiled. "Should I be flattered by your interest?"

"Absolutely not," Lucy responded with exaggerated gaiety.

He stepped nearer to Margaret. "I'm unsure of my holiday plans, but apparently that makes two of us."

And our child makes three. Margaret gasped aloud. Now where had that thought come from? The silence stretched, as the seconds ticked by.

Fernando turned to her. "See you soon. You'll love Antonio's. The pizzeria hasn't changed." His fingertips slid lightly along the edge of her hairline, and he pressed a quick kiss to her forehead. "This holiday is turning into more of a celebration than I ever dreamed."

She swallowed. And more of a disaster than she'd ever imagined.

～

"WHAT ARE YOU DOING?" Lucy demanded as soon as Fernando's footsteps had retreated down the hallway and the front door slammed.

Margaret pointed at Lucy. "You're the one who let him barge into my office."

Lucy put her hands on her hips and stood straight to her full height of five feet. "And you're the one who agreed to see him again!"

"You know he'd never leave me alone until I consented. One night, a brief dinner, and he'll be satisfied."

"When it comes to you, he's insatiable. I saw the way he still looks at you."

Margaret shook her head. "Not anymore. We're all grown up."

"He loved you enough once to want to marry you. How will we ever hide Amelie from him?"

"We've done a good job these past five years."

"Yes, when we were separated by three thousand miles. But here in the same town, it's impossible. You should've told him years ago." She shook her head and sighed deeply. "I knew we never should've returned."

"We didn't have a choice. I'm paying bills and plan to buy back my old trailer."

"Why? We need the money for more important things like rent and food."

"I was fortunate that my former agency set up this winter-wonderland gig for me just when California was so uncertain. They've taken care of all the expenses at the mall and the office and I'll still make money. When I learned about the foreclosure a couple of months ago, I knew I needed to return for a few weeks."

"That rusty old thing has probably disintegrated. What are you trying to prove?"

That she no longer was the needy, poverty-stricken girl who lived at the end of Spruce Street. But she didn't say her belief aloud.

"Fernando doesn't suspect a thing," Margaret assured Lucy. "Besides, he doesn't know our home address. Amelie will attend school while we work in the office during the day, and we'll be gone in six weeks."

"He found your office."

"Coincidence. He didn't know I was working with this agency again."

Lucy shook her head. "He always had a bloodhound sense when it came to you."

"But he missed the most important part, his daughter." Margaret fished in her tote for her car keys. "Did my LA agent call? There's another casting for a drama starring some very famous actors."

"Nope."

Margaret pushed aside the thought of not booking any more jobs in Hollywood. People had short memories, and one blockbuster film was a matter of one successful audition.

"I'll see you tonight at the apartment after I pick up Amelie from school and stop at the grocery store. I want to try a new recipe for stuffed peppers."

"You're becoming domesticated?"

"I'm changing my life for the better, remember?"

As long as it wasn't German food, she could manage anything.

CHAPTER FOUR

F ernando stepped into the icy wind and pulled his scarf tighter around his face. The wind blew horizontally, whirling around him as he strode toward his metallic-silver Mercedes. He limped part of the way, hunched over, and caught his breath. This damn ceaseless pain. He should've been fully recuperated by now.

A homeless man huddled beneath a store awning extended an empty can. Fernando reached in his pocket for the spare one dollar bills he always carried and deposited several. Then he continued walking.

Conscious of Lucy's exasperated expression, he hadn't hesitated when he'd left Margaret's agency, hadn't even glanced back. It was amazing the willpower he'd exhibited at seeing her again. She was more beautiful now than when she was eighteen years old, and he'd longed to hold her in his arms and never let go. How was it possible her skin stayed so perfectly white in California and her cheeks so rosy? He swallowed the lump in his throat as he pictured her trim form and the brightness in her expressive hazel eyes. She'd chewed her bottom lip when she'd told him Christmas wasn't a joyful time for everyone. Her lips were so red, so moist, so desirable. She'd looked incredibly gorgeous in her silk blouse, her figure slender and yet voluptuous. She'd twined her arms around him as if they'd hadn't been separated for six years.

Jacob, an old friend from high school, was getting out of a car as Fernando walked past. Clad in a T-shirt and jeans, Jacob was apparently unaware of the blustering wind. He gazed in the car door mirror and slicked back his hair. Then he folded his enormous arms across his chest and leaned against the car. He was reported to have been an excellent policeman before he'd been thrown off the force for misconduct. Some said he was over-the-top abrasive when arresting people.

"Good to see you again," Jacob said. "How's your brother?"

Although irritated at the interruption of his thoughts of Margaret, Fernando gave a brief nod. "He's much better. Thanks for asking."

"And you? Word from a nurse friend of mine was you were sicker than your brother after the operation."

"Just a rumor." That was the trouble with small towns. People made it their business to know everyone else's business.

"I'd always pegged you as a hockey jock. You're okay with one kidney, right?"

"Couldn't be better." Fernando tried not to hold his waist. The throbbing assaulted him abruptly at the most inopportune times.

"You won't have problems with one kidney later on?"

"Shouldn't."

"My grandmother only has one lung," Jacob called over his shoulder as he started walking in the opposite direction.

"Then your grandmother and I share a common bond. One lung, one kidney."

Jacob apparently hadn't heard because he kept walking.

When Fernando reached his car, he clung to the side door and almost doubled over. Surely this pain would subside soon.

His brother had needed a kidney. When he'd learned he was the logical donor, he'd volunteered without hesitation. His kidney allowed Michael the opportunity to live a normal life free from dialysis. The doctors gave Michael a life expectancy of only thirty years because of his dwarfism and resultant medical issues. Fernando shook his head and squeezed his eyes closed. What did doctors know, anyway? Michael was going to live to be one hundred.

He settled into his car, turned on the engine, and rested his hands on the steering wheel. The needling ache tore at his insides. He pulled the vial from his shirt pocket, grabbed a bottle of water in his glove compartment, and swallowed a yellow pill. His thoughts focused on Margaret, his stunning princess. Clearly, she hadn't expected him. Her eyes had widened when he'd entered her office, and for the first time in her life she'd appeared speechless-- not the response he'd hoped for. Once upon a time they'd planned to celebrate the Christmas after high school graduation as husband and wife. A Christmas wedding, her resplendent in a winter-white velvet gown and carrying a bouquet of deep red roses, a tiara in her hair. Sure, he'd done most of the planning, but she had agreed, hadn't she? She'd called him Prince, adding a different name depending on the circumstances of the day—Prince Polite, Prince Pleasant, he'd heard them all.

And then she'd left him. It was as if she'd slapped him across the face, when in reality the hurt hadn't set in immediately. He'd been a damn, besotted fool. The first letter he'd written her after she'd left him cold was filled with outraged pride. The others had been demanding and then pleading, something he never thought he'd do.

His thoughts flew back to their senior year, when he'd

asked his hockey buddies to clear tires and debris from her front lawn one Saturday afternoon. When he'd stepped into her trailer's run down foyer and inhaled the smell of stale cigarettes, he'd had to push unexpected tears from his eyes. She'd been furious, shouting at him to be a man, not a baby. Her life didn't bother her, so it shouldn't bother him.

But it did bother her.

He'd seen the shame in her face and the sheen of tears and had realized the humiliation she must have felt. And he knew, even then, that she was extraordinary and he didn't deserve her. She was as precious as a rare diamond, and he'd wanted to keep her close and safe. Otherwise, he might lose her. And she'd left. He'd lost her. A year passed before he'd placed his feet back on the ground and decided to move forward without her.

And then he'd heard she was back in town.

He exhaled a pent-up breath, full of pain, and popped another pill. He folded some extra napkins neatly into the glove compartment and put the car in gear. Slowly, he drove toward his real estate management office.

With the excuse of filling out an application for Michael, he'd planned to tell her that her old trailer and the trailer park were being foreclosed upon and that he was purchasing both. Since she hadn't lived in Owanda for years, she wouldn't care.

He leaned back against the leather seat as he drove, the road ahead of him freezing up. He was compulsive about arriving ten minutes early for every appointment and drove well below the speed limit because he always allowed himself extra time.

He'd hoped his gift would bring her gladness, a reminder of happier times, but she hadn't bothered to open it.

CHAPTER FIVE

As usual she was running late. Margaret steered her small white Volvo around the narrow country roads and forced away the thought of Fernando's unexpected appearance. She'd wanted to launch into a tirade about his perpetual planning before he'd smothered her words with a kiss. His hands had caressed her back while pulling her close to him. They fit together intimately-- they always had-- and she knew he'd guard her with his life. He'd gazed at her with unbearable tenderness. Seeing him again, she realized how much she'd missed him, his indulgent smile and silent strength.

She chewed her bottom lip. What was wrong with wanting to feel needed and loved? She glanced out the side window at the cloudy skies and endless precipitation. Nothing, for the average woman living in Owanda. But not for her. If she ever married she'd be a full partner. She wasn't looking for a lord and master who believed he could make all the decisions because he controlled the paycheck.

She gripped the steering wheel and kept her gaze on the

road. The sleet had stopped, and she pulled the car up to the curb at precisely three o'clock, just as the school bell rang. She got out and soon spotted her daughter racing toward her from the building.

"Mom! I love school! And I didn't cough once!" Amelie's voice was a loud monotone as she ran to the car. Her small form was dwarfed by her new berry-red parka and the sparkly polka-dot book bag on her shoulders She carefully carried a tiny white kitten. "Look what my teacher said we could have. It's a boy and he only has one eye."

Margaret stared at the kitten. "So cute, but we can't keep him. We're only here until the end of December and don't have room for anymore rescue animals in our small apartment."

Her daughter's mouth quivered, and she plopped a kiss on the kitten's forehead. "We had lots of strays in California, and you said a kitten is almost as good as a daddy."

Margaret shook her head. Opening the car door, she pushed some office supplies off the front seat onto the floor and placed the kitten on the seat. "This isn't California and I never remember saying that."

"All the other kids in my class have a daddy, but mine can't live with us, right?"

Amelie brought up the most sensitive subject when least expected.

Margaret blinked back threatening tears and braced her hands against the car door for support. "No, he can't. He's ... busy."

"Will he come back someday?"

"Remember how much I love you. Daddy not living with us isn't your fault. There're all kinds of families, and our family is you and I and Lucy."

"And our new kitten." Amelie jutted out her small, determined chin. "I know Daddy will come back some day."

Leave it to a child to display unguarded optimism. Margaret regarded her daughter with heartbreaking admiration. She had such resilience. She tucked Amelie in the backseat and pulled matching berry-red insulated mittens on her small hands, then buckled the seat belt. She placed the book bag on the floor.

"Let me speak with your teacher," she both signed and spoke. Amelie was hard of hearing and wore a hearing aid. Margaret always made eye contact with her daughter, as Amelie relied on visual cues and gestures as well as lip-reading and signing.

Mrs. Henderson, the kindergarten teacher, waddled over. Her crop of wiry-gray hair was pulled back in a messy bun. Her beige wool coat was buttoned securely around her large body.

"The first day went well?" Margaret spoke aloud while signing so Amelie was included in the conversation.

"Very well." Mrs. Henderson glanced at the front seat. "Can you take the kitten home? I found him on my front step this morning, and your daughter told the class you took in strays in California. My mother lives with me and is allergic to cats, or I'd keep him. With only one eye, this kitten has a slim chance of being adopted if I take him to a shelter."

"Please, Mommy?" Amelie offered her most persuasive smile. And the kitten was already curled up and sleeping in the front seat.

"We already have Grumpy," Margaret argued.

"Grumpy needs a friend," Amelie signed.

"A parrot doesn't necessarily want a kitten for a friend."

"Grumpy is safe in his parrot cage. Please, please, Mommy?"

Margaret sighed. "All right, but I can't commit for a long period of time."

"Yay! I knew you'd say yes!" Amelie signed, and then

thoughtfully nibbled at a pencil she'd retrieved from her book bag. "What should we name him?"

"You always come up with the greatest names." Margaret smiled at the memory of the three-legged dog they'd rescued in California. Amelie had named him Tricycle.

"Sounds like you have a kind heart for animals." Mrs. Henderson laughed and handed Margaret a small folder. "She made several new friends. You may be arranging playdates by this weekend."

Margaret grinned. Playdates. A normal life so different from Hollywood. Her intelligent, courageous daughter, despite her desperate shyness, had bravely attended a new school, and the kitten would help the adjustment to Owanda. Margaret ran a bare hand along the thin layer of snow on the car door, the cold hardly registering. If her daughter was in high spirits, then working in this wintry, freezing town and adopting a one-eyed kitten was the right decision.

She smiled at Mrs. Henderson. "Amelie suffered from several bad colds in California, but the cold weather here has agreed with her." With a quick wave, Margaret got into the Volvo and drove off.

The weatherman had predicted lake-effect snow by evening, but he was wrong because heavy snow accumulated on the windshield during the drive home. Snow-covered pines lined both sides of the narrow road, and the windshield wipers made loud slaps while rhythmically pushing the soggy snow back and forth. She blasted the heater and defroster, allowing a small area to peer through.

"Can someone please remind me why anyone in her right mind would want to live here permanently?" she asked aloud as she slowed the car to a crawl. Next year she'd rent a car with four-wheel drive so she could get better traction. She grimaced and shook her head. Umm, no, there'd be no next year in Owanda. Amelie's private school in California was holding her spot, and another tuition payment was due in January.

"Mommy, what did you say about living here?" Amelie signed.

She offered her daughter a bright smile. "Nothing. We'll be home soon, cutie." She glanced at the sleeping kitten and turned up the car radio as a soothing guitar arrangement of "Good King Wenceslas" came on. Amelie hummed gaily and off-tune from the backseat.

A few minutes later, Margaret pulled into her driveway and let out a slow, deep breath. She hadn't driven on icy roads in California.

Lucy, wearing a cotton-candy pink sleeveless dress with a canary-yellow wool coat pulled over her head, stepped unsteadily out of their brick apartment. She waved a snow-brush in the air like it was a new invention. Thick snowflakes danced around her petite body. A picture-perfect holiday scene marred by the fact she wore black patent leather stilettos, and the large tattoo of a clock emblazoned on her forearm didn't look the least bit Christmassy. "Did you stop at the grocery store for peppers?"

Margaret rubbed her forehead. "I forgot. So much for my first day of domesticity." She reached for the kitten and got out of the car. "Does a one-eyed kitten count?"

Lucy put a hand to her heart and dropped the snowbrush. "Isn't a deaf parrot enough?" She teetered precariously to the car, examined the kitten, and frowned. "Hopefully he won't need expensive trips to the vet."

"Isn't he perfect?" Amelie unbuckled her seat belt and dashed from the car. She snatched the kitten from Margaret's grasp and held him close to her chest. "Maybe our kitten can be a doctor someday so we won't have to pay for the vet visits. We'll name him Doc!" She spun in a half circle. "I love Owanda!"

Her happiness was so infectious that Margaret's smile warmed. Perhaps California sunshine and balmy weather was overrated.

CHAPTER SIX

"Darling, you've been twirling that water glass around this entire meeting." Diana's high voice jarred Fernando back to the plush boardroom. "Did you hear what my father said?"

Fernando straightened the wooden coaster and set down his glass. He neatly folded the white cloth napkin beside it.

"Every word." In truth, his thoughts were filmy, and time moved slowly. He shouldn't have taken the second pill. He had a high threshold for pain, but the operation had left him more tired and weaker than he'd anticipated. He fought through the fog, looked at his watch, and tried to gauge the time. *Focus*, he told himself. This was important.

"If you two lovebirds are finished whispering, we'll get back to finalizing this deal." Scott Jackson, Diana's father and the wealthiest man in several Florida counties, smiled approvingly from the opposite end of the long glass table. He was closing in on seventy, and his face looked oddly smooth and shiny and free of wrinkles. Plastic surgery was a wonderful thing.

"Sorry, Mr. Jackson." Fernando squinted at the fluorescent lights glaring from the ceiling and making his head pound. "Your daughter distracted me."

"Perfectly fine. We're through for today. I've talked enough about business and am ready to head home." Scott slid back his chair. "Once the auction is finalized and the sale price agreed upon, the only distraction you'll need to concern yourself with is where to spend all your money. But if I know my daughter, it'll be an easy task."

Fernando offered a half-hearted laugh. "I appreciate your assistance in financing this real estate deal. An outlet mall requires a lot of capital."

Scott's forehead creased, or tried to. "Those trailers should've been torn down years ago. My investors and I are doing this decrepit town a favor. It's been stuck in a time warp. Think of all the new jobs we're creating."

He stood, and Fernando did as well, striding over to Scott and extending his hand. He forced a smile as the men shook hands. "Thank you for your generosity," Fernando said.

"I believe in winners. You're diligent and skilled in this business, and your instinct is good for sound investments. As soon as you move permanently to Florida, there are several other properties we can develop together. I guarantee your real estate business will double within the next year."

Beneath the tan and trimness, Scott appeared much older close up, Fernando noticed.

"Thank you, sir."

"My daughter's a lovely girl. She's all I have, and I'd give her the world."

Fernando gave a brisk nod. That statement was as loaded as it got.

Scott offered a genuine smile in her direction. "I'll wait for you in the foyer, Diana."

"I'll only be another minute, Dad."

Fernando figured she'd likely be much longer, but she was used to people waiting for her. The two of them watched as Scott exited.

"Dinner at my place tonight?" Diana asked. She followed Fernando back to the table as he arranged the paperwork into one bundle. She didn't have a head for business, only pleasure, and he knew where the conversation was headed. An exquisite meal, a bottle of wine, and then he'd spend the night. Under her attractive demeanor, she was ruthless when it came to getting what she wanted. He'd witnessed her negotiation skills in action when she'd purchased her current home near the Atlantic Ocean. She had wanted all the expensive paintings the owner had collected through the years, and she'd gotten them. The owner hadn't stood a chance.

"Angelina, my housemaid from Florida, is broiling sirloin steak with roasted potatoes and chocolate pie for dessert. In the morning, Dad and I will be returning to Florida, so it'll be the last time I see you for a few weeks."

He placed a hand over where his kidney had been removed. "I can't. I'm more tired than I anticipated."

"You never should've donated one of your kidneys. Just because Michael's your brother doesn't mean you owe him anything."

"It was a privilege, not an obligation."

"He could've waited on the list for a donor."

He held up a hand. "I'll not argue anymore about this."

"But are you all right? You've lost weight since the operation."

"I'm here, aren't I? And yes, I'm fine."

But he was the opposite of fine. He lifted a dismissive shoulder, reached for his water glass, and took a sip. He placed the glass back on its coaster and wiped at the water spots on the table with the folded napkin. "I'll meet you at the airport in the morning to see you off."

She didn't look happy but went into satisfied mode. Lowering her voice, she asked, "Are you taking the pills my doctor prescribed? I didn't tell him they were for you. They're magical, aren't they? Let me know when you need a refill."

He nodded, patting the pill bottle in his shirt pocket. "I needed a few to get me through a rough time. I didn't heal as fast as I thought."

"You work too hard and never take any time off." She touched his hand, close to his abdomen. It was an intimate gesture. Her hands were smooth because she'd never done a day of manual labor. Who flew in their housemaid from Florida, anyway?

"When you relocate permanently to Miami, you can relax and spend your days sailing with Dad and me."

"I can't leave my mother to look after my brother by herself, as her eyes are starting to fail and she doesn't drive anymore. Besides, Michael's condition could worsen at any time."

"He rented his own apartment until you demanded he move back with your mother."

"He wasn't well and couldn't be alone."

She shrugged. "Your family will understand your life is in Florida with me. They can manage on their own and we'll hire in-home care. You can commute between Miami and Owanda."

"I won't fly. I tried it once and vowed never again. Must be the air pressure."

She laughed. "A flight from Florida to New York State takes less than three hours. Sit in first class, enjoy a couple of drinks, and you'll be fine."

"I'll take an overnight train," he said. "Besides, I like this town and don't want to leave it permanently. It's home."

"Then you'll have two homes. But this holiday you

promised to spend Christmas in Florida and stay through New Year's."

"Of course." He glanced at his watch. He didn't belong here.

She was his fiancée. She was supposed to act interested and loving. So was he.

Her crystal-blue gaze searched his. "Tell me that's what you want. We'll take trips to Europe after we're married."

"Of course." Same response, with an even more incredulous tone, as in "How can you possibly think otherwise so please stop asking."

She sighed an exaggerated sigh. "Sorry your brother can't withstand long trips. It's better if he stays here with your mother."

She didn't look at all sorry, and he knew she'd never had compassion for sick people. Sometimes he had the feeling she only put up with his family to please him.

He squeezed her hand. "I'll take an early morning train to Florida on Christmas day."

"Good. We'll celebrate Christmas night on Dad's sailboat." She smoothed her hand across his shirt sleeve. The two-carat diamond in her engagement ring flashed in those damn fluorescent lights. He'd spent a fortune on it after her father had contributed a substantial amount of money to his real estate venture in Florida. The shopping center and apartment complex had proven a success.

He gazed at her platinum-blonde hair, her tiny turned-up nose. She was a lovely woman, and she cared about him. Sure, he was her rebound fiancé after her former lover had left her at the altar. At least, that was the story she'd told, although it had changed several times. Still, they respected each other. She was exactly who he deserved, persistent and aggressive. Besides, no one married for love anymore.

He assumed she'd drop her hand, but she gripped tighter. "What do you want for Christmas, darling?"

The room fell silent.

He brushed a polite kiss on her cheek. "Nothing special."

She jerked her hand from his sleeve. He blamed his non-answer on his fuzzy brain, although he knew what she wanted him to say. He just didn't say it.

CHAPTER SEVEN

I f ever a person wanted to be humiliated, standing in the middle of the local mall dressed as an elf on Black Friday was the perfect place to do it. Margaret's insides cringed. She'd vowed never to be put in a position of feeling awkward and uncomfortable again, but the ever-present need for money forced her to do embarrassing things.

"Santa, you must wear your beard at all times." She applied eyelash glue to Gus Stefano's chin. He was the local plumber and part-time Santa. She waited several seconds for the glue to become tacky, then pressed the white beard onto his chin until it stuck firm.

He took a long pull from his mug. "This beard itches and the glue doesn't hold properly."

She wiped her sticky fingers on her red velvet pants. Wisps of white beard stuck to her thighs. "If the beard falls off in one of the children's hands, you'll never work as Santa in this town again."

"No kid should be pulling on my beard," Gus said. "If they do, I'll threaten that Santa won't bring them any toys."

"You won't do any such thing. Laugh like a jolly fellow and

say 'ho, ho, ho.'" She tightened the shiny black belt around her emerald-green elf's jacket. One of the seven elves she'd hired had called in sick, so she'd stepped in. Technically the men weren't elves, they were merely short in stature. Michael was the only dwarf.

She glanced at the large mall clock as it chimed nine o'clock. The elves were all late on their first day of work.

Amelie and Lucy were at the apartment baking Christmas cookies, although Lucy would never actually eat a cookie because she was always counting calories. They'd spent several evenings perusing recipes and had decided on three favorites: a peanut butter with a chocolate kiss in the center, a round cookie made almost exclusively of butter, and home-made chocolate fudge. When Margaret returned home, the kitchen would be warm with the aromas of sugar and chocolate.

Gus took another sip from his mug. "I'm sixty-four years old and had one heart attack. I should be retired and sitting on a beach in the Caribbean."

"Rumor has it you love this job and would never give it up."

"Rumor has it wrong. These days I tire easily."

"For a guy named Santa, you complain quite a bit. As soon as the mall doors open, you'll be surrounded by children." She stared directly at his mug. "And that better be coffee in there."

"You're bossy for such a pretty elf." He stared at her pointy green shoes. "If people learn a famous swimsuit model is here, you'll be surrounded by a mob clamoring for autographs."

She laughed. "The public is fickle and fans want a new fresh face. I'm yesterday's news."

Gus set his gaze on the mall entrance doors, their glass dusted with snow. A line of shoppers snaked around the building. "Who takes their kids out the morning after Thanksgiving, anyway? My grandkids are at home in their pajamas watching TV and playing games." His blue eyes twinkled. He looked so much like Santa. Despite his gruffness, he had one of the kindest hearts of anyone in the world.

"I'd prefer to stay home in my pajamas too," she said.

That's what made Gus a good Santa. He couldn't come to grips with the commercialism surrounding Christmas, and neither could she. She'd much rather fill her apartment with abandoned stray animals than a roomful of designer dresses.

"Yep," he said. "Every dedicated shopper in America is eager to buy, buy, buy. Some have waited outside the mall all night to be first to snag the best deals."

She tilted her head and eyed his red velvet suit. "How many years have you played Santa?"

He was comfortably leaning back in his chair, his large stomach bulging, and one of the shiny brass buttons on his Santa suit was ready to pop. He set down the mug and adjusted his wire-rim glasses. "Over thirty years."

"Then go take your rightful place on Santa's throne." She led him to a peppermint-striped candy-cane throne in the middle of the holiday display. Two gingerbread houses flanked the throne. Several artificial Christmas trees completed the scene, each decorated with oversized gold and peacock-blue bulbs. A sign above the throne said "Wish." Gus bumped his head on the sign as he took his seat.

"That sign should be mounted higher. Or should I say I *wish* the sign were mounted higher?" He rubbed his head and sighed loudly. "Fortunately, this throne gives me the perfect vantage point to admire your shapely little derriere while you prance around in that elf suit."

"Derriere? Is that a new word in your Santa Claus vocabulary?"

"Perhaps later we can ..."

She shook her head. "Never happen."

"Aren't you interested in older men? I'm divorced and single."

"I've sworn off all men, young, old, and in-between. They're way too much trouble. What's more, I could never date Santa Claus."

"Little Margaret." He smiled good-naturedly. "I'm glad you returned for the holidays. I still remember you as a tall, skinny girl who played hop scotch on the sidewalk."

Her trailer had been dark and narrow. She'd stayed outside as often as she could, despite the typically bad weather. An old tool shed had housed several of her rescue animals.

"What were you running from when you left?" he asked.

She gave an incredulous laugh. "You really don't know? How about my terrible life?"

"I heard Fernando was devastated and searched every-where for you."

She couldn't answer. She hadn't known.

"And what were you running toward?" he asked.

Much harder question. She stood quiet before she answered. "In truth, sometimes I don't know anymore."

Success she'd earned on her own, a shot at fame, a taste of wealth. Had any of it mattered? She'd moved to LA to make a better life for her daughter. But the money had slid from her fingers as she'd attempted to keep up with the mounting bills for health insurance, tuition, and medical treatment for Amelie.

"You were always such a kind child, especially to animals," Gus said.

"I'm not in Owanda on a kindness mission. I need the money to pay my bills."

"I came from nothing too, you know. People like us think money equals peace of mind, but it doesn't."

Her memory drew the cold, empty walls of her childhood

bedroom, and a muscle tightened in her throat. "I'm planning to purchase my old trailer because it's in foreclosure. I'll tear it down and put up a real house, a white bungalow with a red front door."

"Don't forget the white picket fence." He nodded. "Sounds like you're changing your life into a make-believe board game. You can't fix everything in your past by tearing it down and replacing it with a fancier substitute."

She chewed her lower lip but kept her back straight. "Watch me."

She'd been pathetic and poor, but she had succeeded. Some of it was luck, yes, a simple roll of the dice that she had been born attractive. But hard work and ambition had made all the difference. She wouldn't accept failure. And she'd never be poor again.

She picked up his mug to discard the contents and sniffed a suspicious whiff of blackberry brandy.

She frowned. "You told me ..."

"Ho, ho, ho." He patted his large stomach with white gloved hands.

A bell on the garland-decorated clock chimed nine fifteen, and a stampede of shoppers raced through the mall doors and into the brightly lit stores. Several had small children in tow, and they lined up so their children would be the first to sit on Santa's lap.

"Has Santa been drinking?" a flushed woman shouted for everyone in Santa's Wonderland to hear. She juggled a chubby-cheeked toddler in one arm and an older child in the other.

"He drinks only coffee," Margaret lied. She briefly wondered if Gus had hidden the brandy bottle amidst the burlap-wrapped Christmas trees and if she could sneak a swig.

At nine thirty, five short men and one dwarf strode

through the mall and stopped when they reached the edge of the Christmas display.

Michael dabbed his irritated red nose and sneezed. "We're here!" He was thinner and paler than she remembered and sported a short dark beard.

She hugged him. "It's good to see you. I hope you're feeling better."

A familiar deep voice came from behind Michael. "I don't remember receiving that same warm, fuzzy greeting from you. Instead, you demanded to know what I was doing in Owanda."

She stiffened and ignored Fernando. "Thanks for showing up to be Santa's helpers," she said aloud to the elves. "Unfortunately, you're all late."

"You told us to report at nine thirty." Buster, the shyest of the men, stroked his long gray beard and kept his head down.

She propped her hands on her hips. "I said to arrive before the mall opened."

"It's six elves against your word," Fernando said. "Admit you're wrong."

She swung around to him. "Who are you, the elf lawyer?"

He gestured toward the camera at the foot of Santa's throne. He was such a good-looking man, resembling a lean hockey player on the cover of a sports magazine. "I can stay a few hours if you need someone to take pictures. I'm your Prince Helpful offering free labor."

She paused and then nodded. Amelie and Lucy weren't due to meet her at the mall until early evening. "All right. Thanks." She smiled.

"I took a photography class in college." He pulled his cell phone out of his coat pocket and snapped a photo of her.

"Well, then you're more than qualified," came her sarcastic reply. She pointed to the heavy camera. "After you take a photo of each child, I'll ask the parents if they'd like to purchase it for five dollars."

"What do I get in return?"

"Nothing, because you volunteered. I'm already over budget for this project."

He grinned. "Want to take a selfie with me?"

"No." She raised a hand to shield her face. "I'm the wrong subject and not sitting on Santa's lap."

"A man can dream, can't he?" He examined the photo on his phone and grinned before tucking it into his pocket. Then he shrugged off his coat and grabbed the heavy camera. "I'll use an action setting and begin snapping pictures as soon as each child approaches Santa. Some of the best photos occur when the subject isn't posing for the camera because that's when you can see the real emotion on a person's face."

"Thank you, Robert Capa," she said, referring to the world-renowned Hungarian World War II photographer.

An older child holding an oversized rainbow-colored lollipop jumped out of Santa's lap. "I said I want two trucks, not one! That's my wish!"

Gus looked at Margaret and lifted both hands as if to say "It wasn't my fault if he's greedy" as the mother raced after her child.

Margaret sighed. "You missed that shot, Fernando."

He snapped another photo of her. "But I found a much more intriguing subject."

$\sim$

THREE HOURS LATER FERNANDO SAID, "I'm expected at a meeting in town. Sorry, because we make a great team."

"Prince Persuasive is leaving his damsel in dire need?" She picked up a lemon-lime slushy drink left on the floor and discarded it in a nearby wastebasket. "Are you meeting your stockbroker?"

He threw an amused look. "Not today. Call me if there's any problem with Michael."

"Can't Michael drive?" she asked.

Fernando shook his head. "He has his license, but I've never encouraged it. Besides, he can't afford a car."

Michael was in line facing them with several children. His face was flushed as he held out a deck of cards facedown. "Pick a card, any card. I'll show you the card you chose."

"How?" one of the children asked. "You're gonna peek."

Michael winked. "It's an illusion."

"Where did he learn magic tricks?" Margaret asked Fernando.

"He's spent many days in the hospital this past year. I introduced him to a magician in New York City, and he's been perfecting magic tricks ever since. Magic takes skill and technique."

She folded her arms together. "It's not real. It's what you want people to believe while you're diverting their attention elsewhere."

He turned that probing gaze on her again. "People have used diversion in their lives to avoid important topics, especially when they're trying to hide something."

Her breath caught. Surely he didn't know about Amelie. She looked up at him.

A good-natured smirk was planted on his face. No suspicion there. "You have my business card with my phone number?"

"I left it at the agency office." In truth, she hadn't bothered to look at it.

He reached into his saddle-brown leather wallet and handed her another one. His cell phone buzzed. As usual, he ignored it. "I'll pick Michael up in a couple of hours. I'll be at my office if you need me."

He had an office? It certainly added credibility to his incessantly ringing cell phone. With a quick wave to the group, he strode past several boutique stores, pushed open the mall doors, and exited.

She walked to the line of squirming children and impatient parents. "Santa will be with you shortly so show him your best behavior."

"Or we won't get any toys for Christmas," one of the children intoned.

"Something like that." She continued to the group of elves who were straightening the metal poles that held the line in place. "Do you want to arrange half-hour lunch breaks among yourselves?"

Michael smiled up at her. "We can stagger the breaks so there're always several elves available in case it gets busier."

Buster glanced in Michael's direction. "He should go first. He's turning white."

She turned. Dear heavens, Michael was swaying on his feet as he limped toward her. Her hands stopped their straightening. "Michael! What's the matter?"

"I'm a little tired." He dropped the deck of cards and held his side. Someone else had done that recently. Someone else had limped and held his side.

Her breath caught in her throat. Fernando, the day he'd left her office. He'd said it was a sprain because he'd been working on his car.

Michael stumbled toward her. "My brother should take me home."

She caught his shoulders. "He left a short while ago. Don't you remember? You waved to him."

Michael picked at invisible lint on his elf suit and

smacked his lips. His gaze had turned wild. So strange to see his eyes bulge. "Where did he go?"

"He went to his office." Although what could be so pressing in any office the Friday after Thanksgiving was beyond her.

Michael twitched in her arms. "I need him." He wrenched from her grasp and dashed through the line of children, knocking over several metal poles.

"I'm dreaming of a white Christmas ..." piped through the mall's speakers amidst the screams of several toddlers. She fumbled for her cell phone. Hadn't Fernando handed her his business card? Her hands shook as she dialed 911 and ran toward Michael. His limbs convulsed, and he collapsed on the floor, taking one of the large Christmas trees into the aisle with him. The silver bulbs shattered. Blood spurted from a gash near his temple. She pressed the cell phone close to her ear and knelt beside Michael. "Answer, someone please answer," she whispered.

Michael gave a puzzled look. "Who are you?"

She tried to wipe the fear off her face. "I'm Margaret. You've known me since you were little."

Gus knelt beside her. "You'll be all right, Michael." He appeared so calm while her heart was pinging a loud beat in her chest.

Gus pulled off his white gloves and Santa Claus hat and propped them beneath Michael's head as a pillow. Then he loosened the top buttons of Michael's green tunic and nudged him onto his side.

"He's having a seizure," he whispered to Margaret. "But don't worry, he's okay. Take a deep breath."

Her heart flip-flopped as her throat constricted. A blank dial tone buzzed in her ear.

She gripped the sleeves of Gus's Santa suit. "My 911 call

didn't go through." She shook her head. "I can't even dial three simple numbers correctly."

"We can't be good at everything." Gus met her gaze. "This seizure shouldn't last more than a couple of minutes. No need to call an ambulance because I'm trained as a paramedic."

Michael's eyes rolled up, his eyelashes fluttered. He was shaking.

"Should we put something in his mouth in case he bites his tongue?"

"Doesn't help. In fact, it might harm him, and we don't want him to break any teeth." Gus surveyed the gawking crowd. "Get rid of these parents and their kids. That'll give you something to do. You're as white as Michael."

She stood on wobbly legs and walked over to the elves. They stared up at her with wide eyes. "Buster, please escort the children and parents away from this area," she said. "Then put up a sign saying we're closed for the remainder of the day."

A security officer strode over to Margaret. He planted himself in front of her, his massive arms crossed over his chest. "Is there a medical problem here?"

"Santa can explain." She pointed to Gus and then walked away to offer candy canes to the children and parents. "I'm sorry but we need to close unexpectedly. Please come back tomorrow." She walked back to Gus and the officer. Michael was standing now, leaning against Gus.

"Yep, everything's okay, officer," Gus was saying. He blinked and patted the officer on the back. "I didn't recognize you at first, Jacob. How are you?"

The officer tilted his head back and rested his hands on his hips. His black short-sleeved polo shirt emblazoned with the word *Security* was too tight for his broad chest. "I got a job at the mall while the police department works on my reinstatement.

You may have read about a drug bust in the newspapers, but I wasn't at fault, just doing my job to get these derelicts off the street." He lifted his shoulders in a semblance of an explanation.

Jacob patted Michael on the shoulder. "And you, little man, shouldn't be working so recently after your operation." He narrowed his gaze on Margaret. "Why did you hire Michael when he's still not well?"

She stepped back. "I was told he'd recuperated and the job would be good for him." She fished in her pocket for Fernando's business card and plugged his number into her cell phone.

"Michael had kidney failure," Jacob said. "Four months ago he received a new kidney from Fernando. You probably know all about it."

She inhaled sharply because in the space of a few seconds, everything came together. The limping, the side holding, the hunching over. The lying by omission. Damn him. How dare he keep this secret from her? She fumed as she dialed his office number. His gold-embossed business card read, "Fernando Brandt, real estate broker, commercial and residential."

A woman answered. "Brandt Realty."

"Fernando Brandt, please."

"Who should I say is calling?"

"Margaret Snow."

"He's in a meeting."

This man had more meetings than the president. "Tell him it's urgent."

His voice came on the line a few seconds later. "Margaret? What's the matter?"

"Michael's suffered a seizure but he's coherent."

"When? Why didn't you call me sooner?"

"It happened so fast. Fortunately Santa's a paramedic."

"I'm on my way." He hung up the phone so quickly, she stared at it for a full ten seconds, outraged, before heading back to the elves. Fernando was beyond arrogant if he believed he could pick and choose what he told her to suit his purposes.

Michael was now sitting on Santa's chair. Jacob, Gus, and the elves surrounded him. "Fernando shouldn't have left on my first day of work." He gazed at her with sweet, soulful eyes, so much like Fernando's and Amelie's that her heart squeezed. She bent to pick up the deck of cards scattered on the floor and handed them to him.

"He's coming very soon."

Jacob stared openly at her. "Hey, you're Margaret Snow. Don't you belong in a magazine wearing a bikini?"

"I'm sorry, do I know you?" She gazed up in the air as if she were checking for the answer on the ceiling. In reality, she was searching for an escape from another lecherous fan.

He slicked back his streaked blond hair. "We were in English class together, sophomore year. I always thought you were the prettiest girl in high school. Wow! Wait till I tell the guys Margaret Snow is in town." He openly perused her, no shyness there. "Great polka-dot bikini you were wearing on the cover of that magazine. Remember the song, 'She wore an itsy bitsy teeny weeny ...'? The guys used to tease Fernando with that song when we'd see him. He let a gorgeous gal sneak off right out from under him."

"One of Bobby Darin's greatest hits."

Her ears burned, and she avoided his gaze. Her agent had urged her to pose for the shoot in the tiniest bikini she'd ever seen, saying it was a stepping stone for her career. She'd dieted and exercised furiously for two weeks beforehand, avoided carbohydrates like the plague, and at times imagined she'd turned into a salad topped with a can of tuna fish. (Packed in water, of course.) When her weight hadn't plunged as much as the swimwear company wanted, she'd taken laxatives. The laxatives had worked to help her shed the last five pounds, but her health had paid for it for months afterward. Lucy had dieted along with her, although Lucy's weight had never returned to normal. She remained stick thin.

"Let's get together," Jacob said. "I've always wanted to try acting. Can you get me an audition with one of your big-time agents?"

"Sorry, I'm very busy." Her theme song for deterring men.

One of the elves caught her gaze. "Do we get paid for today?"

"Yes, of course."

Really? she asked herself. How? With no more money being generated by photos, she'd be forced to borrow from the little savings she had to cover payroll. And that money was reserved for the foreclosure.

"I'll take care of all the wages," Fernando said.

She spun around. "How do you appear out of thin air?"

Smiling, he put his hands in his pocket, pulled out his checkbook, and signed the top check. He tore it out and extended it to her. "I opened the mall door and walked in. You were preoccupied with mall security."

She struggled to keep her anger in check and locked her hands behind her. "Thank you but I can't accept your money."

He grabbed her hands and placed the check in one of them. The smile disappeared. "I insist. I realize you're a wealthy woman, but give the elves a raise if you don't know what to do with all your money."

He didn't wait for her response and started toward Michael. She tucked the check in her pocket and followed him. She'd tear it up later.

Fernando placed his hand on Michael's shoulder. "I heard you were the center of attention today."

Michael sipped from the insulated cup of coffee he was

holding. "I was more tired than I thought. Gus helped because he's a paramedic."

"Thank you." Fernando extended a hand to Gus, and the men shook. "I'll take my brother home now." He turned to Margaret. "Why didn't you call me sooner? I gave you my cell number twice."

"I misplaced your business card."

He let out an exasperated breath. "Does my family mean so little to you?"

She forced herself to meet his gaze. "I'm sorry. I panic in an emergency, and there's a lot on my mind."

"How could I possibly forget how busy you are?" It wasn't a question laced with understanding.

"And how can I possibly forget how manipulative you are?"

"What's that supposed to mean?"

She pushed out a breath in frustrated impatience. "Why didn't you tell me you donated one of your kidneys to Michael?"

He slipped his hand around her forearm and held tightly as she tried to pull away. "We discussed more important topics in your office because we hadn't seen each other in over five years. I expect you to be more understanding."

She wrenched from his grasp. "You expect the world to turn as you planned."

Jacob strode over and laser-tagged his gaze on Margaret. "I'm off work tomorrow. How about dinner at Antonio's?"

A muscle tightened in Fernando's jaw. "Sorry, she's already committed for that restaurant."

"Don't speak for me," she said.

Jacob raised a bleached brow. "I didn't realize you two were still an item."

"We're not," she and Fernando said at the same time. If she weren't so angry, she might've laughed.

Fernando turned and draped an arm around Michael's shoulders. "My car is parked by the entrance. Can you walk a little way?"

"Margaret, let's plan on the Royal Palace for egg rolls," Jacob was saying. "We can check out the Gentleman's Paradise Club afterward."

As she watched Fernando and Michael walk slowly toward the mall exit, she opened her mouth to tell Jacob she'd never be sharing egg rolls with him at the Royal Palace or any other palace, but then she saw Lucy and Amelie enter the mall. They walked directly toward Fernando and Michael, and the four all stopped and greeted one another.

Margaret swallowed and resisted the urge to dash toward them and pull them apart. Time ticked by. Fernando smiled at Amelie, bent down, and began signing. Their hands moved rapidly. Amelie's head tilted up, and Michael joined in the conversation. Lucy walked away, apparently lured by a designer purse sale.

Margaret's breath caught. Surely Lucy wasn't leaving them alone.

Fernando laughed aloud, mussed Amelie's hair and straightened. From across the mall, his probing gaze locked with Margaret's. He nodded.

Her heart stopped, just for a moment. Then it started beating again.

CHAPTER EIGHT

Margaret was aware of Lucy's gaze boring into her back. She whirled and blinked twice, their secret signal. "What's going on?"

Lucy didn't blink back. She gestured toward the small crowd. Amelie scampered off to sit on Santa's throne. "I was going to ask you the same question."

"You go first," Margaret said.

"We finished baking cookies earlier than we anticipated, and I inhaled at least two thousand calories just by sniffing the air. Doc is sleeping contentedly by the fireplace, and Grumpy is probably perched upside down in his cage. Oh, wait." Lucy put a hand to her forehead. "We have Doc and Grumpy, but we don't have a fireplace."

Margaret took hold of Lucy's shoulders. "Isn't there a more important issue to discuss?"

"Amelie and I met Fernando and Michael."

"So I noticed. And you strolled away while Fernando chatted with Amelie. How could you?"

"Amelie was safe. She was with her father, and he was funny and engaging."

"And now you're giving him secret father tests?"

"He's one of the best-looking men I've ever seen, even by Hollywood standards."

"And that makes him father material? How did you introduce Amelie?"

Lucy shrugged. "He must've assumed she was with me, and he was preoccupied with Michael. Remember when he was madly in love with you?" She hesitated, then added quietly, "Some women wait a lifetime for love and devotion."

"The last man I'd ever want is one who controls every aspect of my life. And your precious Fernando has his own secret. I discovered he donated one of his kidneys to his brother, something he purposely hid from me."

"He was always the type of guy who'd do anything for anyone. Remember how compassionate he was to the people in the homeless shelter? He did a lot of volunteering, serving meals and transporting them to and from the hospital."

Firmly, Margaret shook her head. "Whose side are you on?"

"You don't feel obligated to tell the truth about Amelie, yet you're judging him for donating his kidney?"

Margaret gritted her teeth. "What is it about this town that turns everyone into a psychologist?"

Gus shuffled over with Amelie. "This little girl belong to someone?"

"She's with us." Margaret grabbed her daughter's hand.

His smile was kind and thoughtful. "Well, she's coughing really hard. Better watch that."

Margaret bent to Amelie. "You haven't coughed since we left California."

"Just a cough, Mommy. It'll go away," Amelie signed.

"I assume it's you three ladies living alone while you're here," Gus said. "And kids need a male role model in their lives. If you ever need me, I'll come around. I'm experienced and have grandkids, plus I can build an excellent fort out of Popsicle sticks and cardboard boxes. And"—he winked—"I'm Santa Claus."

"Thanks. I'll keep your offer in mind," Margaret said.

Lucy produced a pair of buttery-yellow leather gloves and fanned them at her cheeks. "The kitchen was blistering while we were baking, and I was getting hot flashes."

"Me too, Mommy!" Amelie waved her face with red mittens.

"I bet ice cream will make everything better, cutie." Holding Amelie's hand, Margaret veered toward Owanda's Creamery, the local ice cream parlor.

"Ice cream is almost as good as a kitten and a daddy, right, Mommy?" Amelie asked.

"Right," Margaret assured her.

Lucy shook her head and followed, pushing open the swinging glazed doors of the creamery. She staked a claim at a small yellow table and three chairs near the entrance. "So, no more photos with Santa today?" She pulled up a chair and drummed her fingers on the wrought iron table. What she really meant was, "How are we supposed to pay the mounting bills?"

"We'll open again tomorrow." Margaret studied the chalkboard menu hanging on an adjacent wall. Thirty ice cream flavors were listed, including twists, sorbets, and custards. "I'll miss Michael. He won't be returning because he's obviously not fully recuperated from his operation."

She turned to Amelie and signed. "Two scoops of peppermint ice cream?"

Amelie nodded. "With chocolate sprinkles."

"And a small caramel cone for me. What about you?" Margaret glanced at Lucy.

"Nothing, thanks." Lucy toyed idly with her gloves. Margaret knew she was too weight conscious to be interested in ice cream, especially after stuffing herself with Thanksgiving turkey yesterday and sniffing Christmas cookies today. Lucy eyed a fashionable women's store across the way. "Won't you meet Michael again when you see Fernando?"

"Fernando's decided I'm insensitive, so I doubt I'll hear from him again." She swallowed. For some reason, her heart hurt when she said that.

"Why not, Mommy?" Amelie signed with one hand while tugging on Margaret's velvet pants with the other. "Everyone likes you because you're nice."

She gave a bitter chuckle. Because nothing she'd ever done had met Fernando's high standards, and she wasn't a nice person. She was weak and money-minded and unlovable. She'd tried being a good daughter, but her parents hadn't cared about her. Her childhood friends except for Lucy were non-existent. She'd always been an unpopular, awkward loner who never fit anywhere.

"Sometimes I'm not a nice person," she murmured.

She'd said too much. Lucy's reproving glare confirmed it.

She'd left Fernando because she wouldn't be restricted to a small town. Although, she admitted with a pang of regret, he was everything a man should be. Decisive, intelligent, and caring. Her heart sank when she thought of telling him the truth about his daughter. Would he ever forgive her, ever understand? He'd seemed so cheerful when he was taking photographs of the children on Santa's lap, engaged and interested in each child.

A woman who'd stood in line with her little girl smiled and waved good-naturedly. Margaret smiled and waved back. Small town living was certainly friendlier than California.

Jacob sauntered to the ice cream parlor's entrance and strode inside. "This is my lucky day. I'm seeing two beautiful women and this cute little girl again in one afternoon." He stared at Amelie and then Margaret. "Who's she with?"

Lucy leaned forward. "Both of us."

"How old is she?"

"Five."

"What's her name?"

Lucy paused and shot a glance at Margaret. "Her name is Amelie."

"Pretty." Apparently satisfied, he set his full white-teethed beam on Lucy. "Do you remember me?"

"Of course." Lucy tilted her head as the reflection of the overhead Tiffany lamp doubled the platinum in her blonde hair. She wore black false eyelashes. Fortunately, she didn't bat them. "You poked me with your pen during algebra class when we were in high school."

He leaned nearer. "Because you copied all my answers."

She actually giggled, aloud, with no embarrassment. "You never studied a day in your life. You sat behind my desk and copied all the answers from me."

"Will you join me for dinner? I always thought you were the prettiest girl in our high school."

Margaret raised her brows. That line sounded familiar.

Lucy grabbed her cell phone from her suede, blazing-pink purse. "I'm free any time and you can text me."

He added his number to her phone contacts. His enormous satisfied grin resembled the Cheshire Cat's.

Margaret sighed. Jacob had asked her to accompany him to a gentlemen's club. Was that the reputation Hollywood had branded on her? After endless auditions, casting calls, and trying to memorize lines, she was known only for a skimpy bikini on a magazine cover.

She glanced at Amelie. She'd taken off her glasses, and her bright shining gaze was focused lovingly on Margaret. She offered her daughter a small smile and cleared the sadness from her throat. If only she didn't need to make so much money to be self-reliant. If only her need to prove herself by being a critically acclaimed actress could be calmed. If only Fernando would forgive her, because she did care about him and his family. And Lucy was right. He'd be a wonderful father.

She pulled in a deep breath. *Pluck that thought out of your mind. Your career would end right here in this worn-out town.*

She stood and weaved through a clump of teenagers with pierced eyebrows to the front counter. She switched her order from a small caramel ice cream to a large peppermint sundae. Then she added whipped cream, hot fudge, and a maraschino cherry. After all, it was the Christmas season. Time for good cheer and celebration.

Jacob stepped in line behind her and tapped her on the shoulder. "She's your daughter, isn't she?"

She whirled. "I'm sorry. What did you say?"

"Amelie. She's your daughter."

"Unless an unemployed cop in New York State has different rules from the ones in California, Amelie is none of your business."

"And I decided I know who the father is."

Deny. Escape. Any Christmas spirit she'd felt was quickly turning to panic. She held firm and erected a cool, inscrutable mask over her features. "No one's interested in your outrageous opinions and decisions."

A merry holiday song played through the ice cream parlor's loudspeaker, but still she heard Jacob's soft voice as she whirled around. "I won't tell. Get me that audition so I can vacate this crummy town and move to Hollywood."

CHAPTER NINE

Snow and hard-driving sleet were the order of the day. Fernando must have forgiven her for any imagined thoughtlessness toward his family because he'd called her office and arranged a date two weeks after Michael's seizure. The visit to see his family was postponed until Michael was feeling better. However, dinner at Antonio's was still on. So here she was amidst the scents of tomato sauce, Parmesan cheese, and freshly ground black pepper. She inhaled deeply with appreciation. She'd been eating California salads far too long.

Fernando stood waiting near the entrance of the tiny pizzeria and escorted her to their table. His gaze and smile were all approval. "You're looking lovely."

"Thank you for politely lying because we both know I'm a wet, bedraggled mess." She raised a hand to her face and shook off the sleet that had settled on her red tartan scarf. Her coal-black eyeliner was probably streaming halfway down her cheeks, and a bad hair day was an understatement.

His light brown hair was damp from the sleet, and he pushed a wavy tendril back from his forehead. He wore snug denim jeans and a navy pea coat, and she grinned at him appreciatively. The good-looking teenage boy had become one of the most striking men she'd even seen. For a moment she was caught in the spell of his persuasive brown eyes.

"You're looking well," she said.

"I feel much better, and the pain has lessened. The doctors told me that it would take several months to fully recover, but I tend to be impatient." A faint smile touched his lips. He leaned toward her, his mouth moving closer to hers. "I would've picked you up at your house."

She looked away. "I live out of town in a very nice rental apartment."

No, it wasn't nice. It was freezing, with cold air seeping through the cracks in the walls. Plus, the roof leaked. She shuddered just thinking about the place. That was the problem with lies. Sometimes, most times, they made her very, very tired.

She'd hoped her LA agent would have returned her call regarding prospective auditions, but her cell phone had sat silent for days. Many of the fashion magazines were scheduling January shoots in the Bahamas for their summer issues. It was not encouraging that her agent hadn't answered her call and hadn't called her back.

Lucy was spending a cozy night at their apartment with Amelie and Doc, the rapidly growing kitten. For a kitten with one eye, Doc was surprisingly mobile. Gus was stopping over to play Go Fish with Amelie.

Tomorrow, Lucy was seeing Jacob again. She'd gone out with him three times, always meeting him in Owanda. She'd become adept at lying, too, and had told Margaret she continued to sidestep his inquiries about Amelie's parents. But how long before Margaret confided in Lucy regarding Jacob's threat?

Fernando tucked Margaret's hand possessively in his and

swept her to a corner table. A small fire crackled in the fireplace. He helped her off with her coat, then shrugged off his own and draped both over their chairs. She hung her purse over the back of her chair and examined the reindeer salt and pepper shakers in the middle of the table.

"This pizzeria hasn't changed. Plastic reindeer are a charming addition," she said.

He laughed. "Much different from your fancy California restaurants. They probably use real fir trees as centerpieces."

She set the reindeer on the table and perched her chin on her hands. "Those restaurants are too health conscious, and I can only eat so much tofu. I used to love Antonio's eggplant."

"I already placed your order. Eggplant parmesan and a side of angel hair spaghetti for you and a double order of the same for me. And we can share a cheese and spinach pizza." He smiled. "I assume you're hungry after working at the mall all day."

This was the part when she was supposed to thank him for remembering the food she loved and being considerate, but instead she bristled and said nothing. He was well-meaning but she had a more accurate description: controlling.

The owner, Antonio, greeted them and filled their water glasses. His white mustache, weathered face, and kind dark eyes made him easily recognizable. "I heard we had a famous swimsuit model in our midst. My little Margaret, still as lovely as ever."

Fernando nodded. "She's perfect."

She shook her head. "I disagree, but thank you." No matter how many times she was complimented, she still saw herself as the awkward, too-thin girl who lived at the end of Spruce Street.

She accepted Antonio's warm hug. He smelled of mozzarella and fresh basil.

"How long are you in town?" he asked.

"I've tried for an answer, but she's mastered the art of evasiveness," Fernando said. "I'm hoping she'll grace my mother's home with a holiday visit."

She squeezed her hands on her lap. Memories of his house at Christmas time came back in a rush. Silver tinsel hanging on pine branches, the scent of butter cookies sandwiched with raspberry jam. Handel's *Messiah*, the grandest of all choruses, sounding from the CD player. And if she entered that house, her heart would break for the family and endless love Amelie had lost. Instead, Amelie had a mother who'd put her Hollywood career above spending time with her daughter. Ironic. She'd wanted to be independent and create a perfect life for her daughter, but she couldn't spend quality time with her because she was too busy working.

And she was still doing it, waiting for her agent's call.

Get your priorities in order.

She sat straighter and willed the chatterbox in her head to stay silent. No recriminations. One big movie role and she'd retire because her money problems would be over.

Antonio took a step back. "Seeing you two together is like old times."

"And old times are the best times." Fernando's gaze met hers, warm with admiration. "Although she's always been out of my league."

Caught off balance by his compliment, she touched the corners of her eyes to catch the tears. He'd been the hockey star, while she was the excluded, dirt-poor outsider. She wanted to say something but knew her voice would break. This town, this man, this eggplant, threatened to defeat her. Her memories had been safely stowed to be brought out at a later time when she determined. But her therapist had been wrong. The memories sprang from their compartment whenever she was within two feet of Fernando.

"Can I get you a bottle of wine, a celebration for two high school sweethearts reunited?" Antonio asked.

She covered her empty wineglass. "None for me, thanks."

Fernando lifted a brow. "Your Hollywood reputation precedes you. Aren't you a party girl?"

She shook her head. "I learned that alcohol isn't my friend. Have you ever heard other friends say they were having problems, and then they started drinking and all their problems disappeared?"

Fernando laughed. "None for me either."

Antonio smiled and walked away.

Fernando reached for her hand across the table, his thumb lightly caressing her fingertips. "You're a good influence."

"My decision isn't necessarily your decision. I know what's right for me."

He smiled at her as if she were extraordinary and precious. He squeezed her hand, his grasp warm and familiar. "And I respect you for that."

She sighed with pleasure. Many of her girlfriends in high school had wanted him at their side to enjoy his popularity and the male strength radiating from him. Yet, he'd wanted only her. He brought her hands to his lips and brushed a light kiss on her palm. A smile of contentment touched her lips. And he still wanted only her.

At the table behind her, a young couple shouted at each other. Their toddler had been playing peek-a-boo with Fernando.

"See that little boy?" he asked. "He's the reason I never want children."

She pulled her hands from his grasp, turned and caught a glimpse of a child with the face of a cherub. She whirled back and placed her professional actress expression on her face. "I'm surprised. I thought you loved children."

"Other people's children."

She picked up her water glass and took a long drink. For a couple of beats her heart felt crushed in a vice. So, she'd been right in never allowing him to know his daughter. She set down her glass and nodded slowly as if she were pondering his words. "Children are a lot of responsibility."

"Do you know why I don't want children?" he asked.

No, no, no. She tried an interested half smile. "Why?"

His face grew serious. "My brother suffers from sickle cell syndrome. It's a hereditary gene and we're twins. Seeing my brother struggle ... Well, I couldn't bring children into the world knowing they might need to fight to survive as he has had to. His life has been a series of hospitals and sickness, and it's been difficult watching him suffer and knowing there isn't anything I can do." Fernando thumbed at the corners of his eyes and looked down.

"Were you tested for the gene?" she asked.

"Yes. And I have the sickle cell trait, which is different from sickle cell syndrome. I don't suffer from any symptoms, and it's not a disease. Just no mountain climbing or scuba diving for me because of the change in oxygen levels." He laughed but didn't sound amused. "However, if my wife had sickle cell syndrome, our children would have a 50 percent chance of having either the trait or the syndrome."

"And if she didn't?"

"Still 50 percent. Besides Michael's dwarfism, the syndrome has resulted in fevers, chest pain, and coughing. But enough about illness. We're here to celebrate our reunion."

She chewed her bottom lip as her mind raced back to the day when Amelie was born. The hospital had checked for sickle cell syndrome, hadn't they? It was a routine test administered to all newborns.

Breathe. Stay calm. She stared into the cheerful flames of

the fireplace and inhaled the scent of wood smoke. Amelie had been born with a hearing impairment, but she deserved every second of life. Margaret couldn't imagine even one day without her precious daughter.

She glanced uncertainly at Fernando.

He gazed back with a look of deep pride, and her heart gave a peculiar little lurch. "I'm proud of all you've accomplished in California. You're extremely smart and courageous and selfless."

She swallowed. He was crediting her with his own honorable traits. He was noble and thoughtful and kind. She placed a hand atop his, and he smiled. There was no mistaking the look on his handsome face. Without a doubt, he still cared.

Behind her, the toddler's chubby fingers pulled on her coat. She spun around as he stood on his chair. Her hands flew out to grab him before he tipped over, but his young mother was faster, elbowing Margaret out of the way while scolding him.

Margaret turned back to Fernando and folded her clammy hands together. "Whew. Close call." She choked out the words. "You name the emergency, large or small, and I panic."

"You reacted quickly. I didn't see that coming and I was facing him," he said.

Because in your effort to control everything, you don't see what's in front of you.

Her eyes clouded. She'd been two months pregnant and had already gained ten pounds when she'd left Owanda. At eighteen years old, her breasts had been heavy, and none of her jeans fit around her waist. She'd been sick every morning before school. Nonetheless, he hadn't noticed. He was one of the most astute people she'd ever known, but he hadn't noticed. And if he had, he would've taken charge and provided for them. She knew him; she knew that. Or maybe she didn't. Her mother had waited for her drunken husband to provide for them, and he never had. Instead, she should've taken matters into her own hands and gotten a job. Even now her mother's hopeless, wistful face haunted Margaret's dreams.

Through the pizzeria's foggy window, a thin sheet of icy snow cast a blurry view on the outside world. The winters were endless here, the cold persistent.

"Who was the little girl with Lucy at the mall?" he asked. "Something about her looked so familiar. Is she Lucy's daughter? She was charming and couldn't wait to tell me about Doc, her new rescue kitten. Lucy said the girl's name was Amelie."

Margaret clutched the base of her water glass as a stab of panic went through her. Lucy had told him Amelie's name? Margaret made a mental note to throttle Lucy when she got home. "I hope you and Amelie had a nice chat," she managed to say.

"You always found at least one stray animal to nurse back to health when you lived on Spruce Street."

The teenage waiter interrupted by placing a large pizza rack in the center of the table, then deposited a piping hot cheese and spinach pizza on the rack. His upper lip was pierced. Face piercings, Margaret thought. It must be a prerequisite for teenagers in this town.

"I remembered you liked spinach pizza as much as I do." Fernando handed her the first slice. "You look beautiful when you eat."

"That's three."

"Three what?"

"Three compliments in an hour." She smiled at him around a bite of pizza. The sauce was exquisite, the perfect blend of spices and comfort.

Her cell phone buzzed.

"Excuse me. I'm expecting a call from my agent." She opened her purse and retrieved a text message from Lucy.

Come home. Amelie has a fever and she's coughing.

When did it start? she texted back.

A few minutes ago, Lucy responded.

Sickle cell syndrome. No, it couldn't be. Margaret's head began pounding. She shoved her plate aside and bolted to her feet. "Something's happened ... at work." She pressed her lips together, knowing her whispered explanation sounded painfully quiet.

She could feel the restaurant patrons watching her. She wouldn't scream. She wouldn't cry.

He vaulted from his chair, and his dark brows flicked up with a measured look. "You're leaving?" He threw some bills on the table. His voice sounded far away.

Her hands shook as she texted. *I'm on my way. Call paramedics.* She grabbed her coat and dashed around tables. She couldn't stop running. Alarm swelled in her throat, and she dragged air into her lungs. This couldn't be happening.

Her phone buzzed. The text message from Lucy read, *I already did.*

CHAPTER TEN

Fernando's fingers grazed her elbow as he took long strides through the restaurant to keep up with her. "Where are you parked?"

At the pizzeria's entrance, he saw the sleet had turned to snow, which flew across the ground and shone silver in the moonlight. Margaret pulled away from him. Her face was flushed and she was breathless. "My car is parked at my office."

"Is that where you're going? To your office?"

Tears sparkled in her eyes. "Lucy texted me. I'm driving back to my apartment."

"Why?"

She twisted her tartan scarf until her knuckles turned white. "Amelie is sick."

His attention was diverted by another text message on her phone. She typed a quick reply and turned away from him. Her pace quickened as snowfall swirled in the street lights. Her footsteps muffled by the snow, her black leather boots left small imprints in the blank white sidewalk.

A traditional red kettle was stationed at the next corner, a shivering volunteer ringing his bell, and Fernando threw some spare bills into the kettle. Then, for the second time, he caught up with her. He studied her stricken features and slid his hand beneath her arm. "I'm parked around the corner. I'll take you home."

She shook her head. "My car is only a few blocks from here."

He tightened his grip and steered her toward his car. "I'm closer."

"No." She jerked away and rushed headlong into the street. Several cars swerved, their horns beeping a loud warning.

Cold air pressed against his skin as he raced across the street. "You're in no condition to drive on these icy roads!" His thoughts circled, searching for some sense to her urgency. "What happened?"

"Amelie needs me!" Without a backward glance, she continued running. Heavy black clouds blocked any light from the moon and stars. The red lining of her coat flashed as she ran, and her ebony waves blew wildly around her face. With lengthy, brisk strides, he closed the distance between them, grasped her shoulders, and turned her to face him.

"That's enough. You're coming with me. I'm sure Lucy has everything under control." He deliberately spoke in a level and authoritative tone.

She threw him a murderous look and jerked back. "Believe me, she doesn't!"

Why was she acting like a raving lunatic?

He grabbed her arm and whirled her around to face him. "I insist I take you home." He was surprised when she stopped arguing, but didn't hesitate to guide her around the block to his car. Reaching for the handle, he opened the passenger door. "Don't panic. I'm certain Lucy is an excellent mother."

Margaret closed her eyes and blew out a breath. "Yes, I'm sure she will be. Someday."

A tendril of doubt settled in his stomach. The cold had taken on a bitter edge, and he shivered. "Amelie isn't Lucy's child?"

Margaret shook her head.

"Is Amelie a stray child you adopted in California?"

Her eyes snapped open. "You're joking, right? You're comparing Amelie to a rescue animal?"

She was certainly protective toward the little girl. Perhaps she and Lucy had raised Amelie from birth. He waited, but then sighed when no explanation was forthcoming. "The faster you get in, the faster we get there."

She flicked a glance toward the sidewalk, as if again considering taking her own car.

"I'll get you home safely and quickly, and Amelie will be all right. I promise." He tipped her face up to his and lightly stroked her shiny black hair. Deep inside, the familiar surge of protectiveness rose. He'd happily strangle anyone who tried to hurt her. That is, if she allowed it, because she'd grown from a shy, uncertain teenager to an independent woman with a mind of her own.

Her eyes were shadowed with alarm. She nodded woodenly. With a resigned slump, she slid in and buckled her seat belt.

He ducked into the driver's seat. "Where's your apartment?"

She expelled a long sigh. Her gaze was riveted to the road. "Old Towne Road. You've lived here all your life, so I'm sure you know where that is. Just drive fast."

CHAPTER ELEVEN

She lived farther out of town than he'd imagined. The only apartments he knew on Old Towne Road were in an old, run-down building. What would Margaret be doing living there?

He glanced at her. She kept her eyes on her phone, but no other text messages came through.

"Bad reception on these country roads," he said. His side hurt again, and he could have used a pain pill, although the pain had subsided, becoming less and less each day. He'd discarded the bottle of little yellow pills when Diana left for Florida, though. He couldn't concentrate with the pills fogging up his brain, and he had found himself becoming more and more dependent on them. Addictions, he'd vowed to himself years ago, would never take hold of his life again.

Margaret sat ramrod straight and sobbed softly. Tears glittered in her beautiful hazel eyes and dampened her long dark eyelashes. She looked vulnerable and desolate. "Drive faster. Please," she said.

He held his breath and pressed the accelerator. Trees and branches heavy with snow whizzed by. The road was dark and snow covered, but in spots ice lurked under the snow, and a couple of times his car slipped across the patches of ice. His cell phone tinged with a text, most likely from Diana. She'd been back in Florida three weeks and had contacted him every day. He glanced down, trying to remember where he'd placed his phone.

Too late, he looked up to a car's headlights shining at him. He swerved. Margaret screamed a warning and clutched the dashboard. He'd drifted several inches into the other lane and narrowly missed the black SUV traveling in the opposite direction. A blast from the driver's horn forced Fernando to overcompensate, but he safely negotiated the car back into his own lane.

He glanced at her pale face. "I'm slowing down. This ice and snow are hazardous."

"If you'd kept your eyes on the road, that wouldn't have happened. A skilled driver would never—"

"I'm doing the best I can. I know this area and we're a couple of minutes away from your apartment."

"Then speed up."

He frowned, pushed harder on the gas pedal, and skidded to a stop in front of her apartment. As he'd suspected, the brick building was low and dingy. Blue and red emergency vehicle lights shimmered in the snow, and several vehicles were parked haphazardly in the driveway.

"Thanks for the ride. Drop me off here and you can leave." Margaret flew from the car and slammed the door behind her.

"The hell I will," Fernando muttered. He parked at the edge of the driveway, closed the distance between them, and firmly placed his arm on her shoulders.

She flashed him a defiant glare. For a moment he thought she was going to physically push him off the small stoop before they entered the foyer.

A squawking parrot hanging upside in his cage, several people talking and laughing, and the television, set to a piercing level, greeted them. Amelie sat curled up on the living room couch with her legs tucked beneath her. Gus sat beside her holding a deck of cards.

It's a Wonderful Life was playing on the television. Fernando glanced over, recognizing the part where George walks back to the bridge where he was going to jump. He pleads to Clarence for his life, and Pottersville once again becomes Bedford Falls.

Margaret rushed to Amelie's side, hugged her, and knelt beside her on the worn carpet. She felt the girl's forehead. "You don't seem warm, thank goodness." Briefly, Margaret closed her eyes and the worried expression on her face relaxed. "Are you coughing?"

Gus placed a card face up on the couch. "Yep. She coughed a couple of times, and I told Lucy not to alarm you. Fevers in kids are common and come and go. To stop Lucy's fretting, I called my paramedic friends to check on Amelie. They're in your kitchen grabbing a short dinner break."

"Go fish!" Amelie placed her card triumphantly on top of Gus's, grinned at Margaret, and signed, "It's just a little cough."

Arms folded, Fernando leaned against the door frame. The African grey eyed him from his cage. A basket of Granny Smith apples and plump oranges sat beneath the cage amidst a pile of animal magazines and a laundry basket full of clothes. Margaret had never been interested in housekeeping, perpetually losing track of time when absorbed with her animals.

Amelie waved and signed, "Hi Fernando. Are you taking me ice skating like you promised? I'm planning to wear my red parka so I won't get cold."

Margaret jumped to her feet and glared at him. "When

was this arranged? Amelie can't go ice skating with you. Absolutely not."

"Why? I'm a former hockey player and I can skate fairly well."

Lucy emerged from the kitchen with Doc snuggled against her chest. "Sorry, Margaret, false alarm. I tried to call you after I texted, but there was no signal." She glanced at Fernando. "What are you doing here?"

"Is that the only question you can ever ask me? You gave Margaret quite a scare."

Jacob emerged from the kitchen carrying a plate piled high with pizza.

Margaret stared at him, looking like she'd been hit across the face. She gave Lucy a long, meaningful look and then blinked twice. "I thought he didn't know where we lived."

Lucy lifted her chin. "He missed me."

Jacob shrugged, his jaw tightening. "I'm here a lot. Lucy's a grown woman and can do whatever she pleases. She knows several agents in Hollywood, so I don't need you, but let's be honest, you didn't plan on helping me anyway." He looked at Amelie, and then at Fernando. "Cute kid, isn't she? Such pretty dark eyes."

"She's adorable," Fernando said.

Margaret's gaze narrowed at Jacob. "Amelie is not part of this conversation."

Jacob's cold gray eyes appraised her before he focused on Fernando again. "Amelie can sign because of her hearing impairment, similar to your brother's. Kind of like a common bond."

Fernando looked intently at Amelie. She shook her wavy light brown hair away from her face, then took off her glasses and rubbed her eyes. Looking at him again, those dark brown eyes gleamed impishly. "Fernando, do you like our new kitten, the one I told you about?" she signed.

He nodded as a shiver of realization skipped through him. "How old is she?"

Margaret looked as if she'd been punched in the stomach, but she answered him. "She'll be six years old soon." Her shoulders stiffened. "Thanks again for driving me. I'll walk you out and get my car in the morning."

His feet were firmly planted on the floor. He stared from Amelie to Margaret. Memories flooded across his mind, the unexplained questions he'd shrugged off. Because he was young. Because he was so certain of their future together, he'd grown complacent. The weight gain he'd never mentioned for fear he'd hurt her feelings. Her sickness every morning before school, which he'd attributed to her staying up late with her rescue animals. Her abrupt departure after graduation. For years he'd been devastated, too blinded by hurt and anger to analyze what was clearly apparent in hindsight.

But not anymore. His heart hammered violently. How could he be so blind?

They locked eyes. Her gaze was steady, though her eyes revealed her exhaustion.

Blood roared through his veins, forcing his heart to pound in his ears. He knew. God help him, he knew. He glanced at Amelie, giggling on the couch, absorbed in her card game with Gus.

"You need to leave," Margaret said. "You're blocking the paramedic truck." She stepped past him and opened the front door.

He clamped down on her hand and dragged her out with him, slamming the door behind them. The frozen night waited, and a tremor rippled through him.

"Is it true—what I'm thinking?" he asked.

She swallowed hard. The color drained from her face. She blew out a long breath and met his gaze. "Yes."

One word. The silence suffocated him. A sudden gust of

freezing wind made him shiver. Pointedly, he dropped her hand and looked away. "Why didn't you tell me?"

She twisted her fingers together. "I wanted to. You know I loved you. It wasn't that."

She'd never answered his letters. Now she finally was telling him she loved him, now that he was seeing her for who she really was—a woman who'd do anything for fame and fortune, even if it meant denying him and his daughter.

"You wanted to, but what, it slipped your mind?"

"I was afraid you'd come for us." She avoided his gaze. "I wanted other things."

He gave a bitter laugh and stared down at her beautiful, anguished face. She'd betrayed his love, his trust, and left him cold. His perfect princess. "We had our life all planned."

She chewed her bottom lip and shook her head. "Your plans."

"It could've been the three of us. I knew you had a hard life, and I wanted to give you something better. I wanted to keep you safe."

Her fists clenched at her sides. "Your idea of saving me was living here in this horrible town and keeping me on your leash."

"I never restricted you."

"You didn't need to because everything was already decided—where we were going to live, what we were going to do. I didn't want a life of being married to a high school hockey coach while I stayed home and baked cookies."

"So you kept my daughter from me. Why? For your glamorous career? What's more important, a child raised in a loving family or your precious money?"

A quiet fury boiled inside him. He'd lost all those years—Amelie's baby steps, the first time she smiled, her first words. So many questions, so much he wanted to know. When had her deafness become apparent?

"We're leaving as soon as this mall job is finished," she said. "I've made a home for Amelie and me in California."

"I'll fight for custody."

Tears sprang to her eyes as she drew a ragged breath. "Try it. You'll never win because you'll never find us."

The front door creaked open, and Amelie skipped onto the stoop clutching her red parka around her. "Mommy, don't yell at him. Jacob just told me that Fernando's my daddy." She extended her arms to him, signing and talking all the while. "I told Mommy you'd come back. Why didn't you tell me? Did you want to make it a surprise?"

"I wanted to make it the best surprise, sweetheart." He picked up her delicate, slim body, smelling of strawberry soap and innocence, and cuddled her close.

She clasped her hands around his neck. Her chocolate-brown eyes sparkled. "Mommy said you couldn't live with us, but now you can," she said in her loud monotone.

He kissed her baby-faced cheeks. "I would've come sooner ..."

"You were busy, Daddy. That's okay."

He sniffled and turned from Margaret with his daughter in his arms because he didn't want Margaret to see him vulnerable. Amelie wiped at his cheeks as his tears flowed. He set the girl down and stared at her charming face, the slight gathering of freckles across the bridge of her nose, her tiny glasses fogging in the cold.

She tugged on his hand. "I've been hiding this under my bed. I didn't want Mommy to see because she gets quiet if I talk about my daddy." She reached into her jacket pocket and held up a crayon picture of a man and woman holding a child's hand. They stood on the edge of a sandy beach gazing at the ocean waves. A parrot was perched on the man's shoulder, and the woman held a cat. A dog with three legs stood beside her.

He swallowed and cleared his throat. "It's beautiful," he signed.

Margaret sank to the edge of the stoop and shook her head. "Amelie. You're such a precious and precocious child." She stared up at the dark winter sky. "Why wasn't I paying attention to what my daughter was saying?"

Fernando didn't answer. He stared at Margaret's profile and saw her bottomless kindness and her misguided and reckless logic. She'd been young and headstrong and imprudent when she'd fled, but she was all he'd ever wanted in a woman. If only she'd desired him as much as he'd desired her. If only she'd allowed him the opportunity to prove that he'd give her everything she deserved.

"You've done a wonderful job raising her," he said.

"Lucy helps." A wry smile grazed Margaret's lips. "Believe me, Amelie's a handful."

He extended a hand to her. A beat went by before she accepted and stood. Mere inches separated them but he didn't pull her closer. "We can work this out together."

Her gaze was proud, her spine straight. "Perhaps."

"For Amelie's sake," he said, "anything's possible."

Amelie had been catching snowflakes on her tongue. "Daddy, listen! Tomorrow we can ice skate and then stop for peppermint ice cream with chocolate sprinkles in the mall." Her hands signed rapidly. "Mommy will be helping Santa, but we can say hi." She tugged on the hem of his coat. "Bend down, Daddy. I have a secret to tell you."

He bent so their faces almost touched. "What is it, sweetheart?"

"That's not the real Santa in the mall," she whispered loudly in his ear. "It's Gus pretending to be Santa. I know because his beard is fake and falls off. And I heard Mommy tell Lucy that Gus drinks too much blackberry brandy, and I can smell it on his breath when he pretends to be Santa."

CHAPTER TWELVE

"Daddy and Mommy, watch me!" Amelie wobbled precariously on tiny white skates and stuck out one leg. Margaret laughed from the bleachers and clapped vigorously. "Be careful," she signed. Fortunately, she'd managed to find an ice skating rink in California and had taken Amelie skating a couple of times.

Fernando, on his own skates a few feet away, added his applause. "Perfect skating today, sweetheart," he signed. "The rink is closing, so let's clear the ice. We can come back tomorrow." He grabbed her hand, and they skated over to Margaret.

Margaret opened her arms and wrapped her daughter in a big hug. "This is your third time ice skating, and you're becoming a wonderful skater! I'm so proud of you."

He deposited Amelie on a bench, removed her ice skates and then handed her several dollar bills. She laced up her furry, hot-pink boots and scampered to the rink's snack bar for hot chocolate and a pretzel.

Ice skates decorated with evergreens and pine cones were

displayed on the rink's bulletin board, reflecting the holiday spirit. *The Twelve Days of Christmas* sounded over the loudspeaker. The air smelled of leather, hockey skates, and stinging cold.

"Our little girl is always hungry," Fernando said, laughing. "Wintry air and vigorous exercise perks up an appetite."

Margaret tipped her head toward him. "Just like her father."

He smiled shamelessly and led her to a corner of the snack bar. She eyed the booth and blinked. "Why are we sitting back here?"

He put his hands in his pockets and shrugged boyishly. "We used to sit in this booth after my hockey practice."

"I well remember."

He glanced at the concession stand. "We can see Amelie perfectly from our booth."

She slid into it, and he settled beside her, the hard muscles of his leg touching hers.

"Our daughter's a natural on the ice," he said.

"Just like her father," Margaret repeated.

"She could be a graceful figure skater, or she could play ice hockey when she gets older. We'll make every opportunity available to her."

Margaret raised her eyebrows. "It's only been two weeks. We're taking this slow, remember?"

Sadness touched his gaze. "I'm thrilled she's in my life, and there's so much I want to give her."

"You're forgetting about my career in California," Margaret said, although exactly what that career entailed she wasn't sure anymore.

With a grim but encouraging smile, he said, "You're an ambitious, successful, woman, and I won't prevent you from pursuing your goals. Nor would I want you to hinder my career."

"Good. We're in agreement."

"And I forgive you."

She flinched. "Forgive me for what?"

He shook his head. "I've pondered and prayed. What's done is done, and I want us to move forward, not backward." He gave her a long, assessing look filled with respect. "Your Christmas display brought you to this town. For whatever reason, be it spiritual or all the stars aligning, I'm forever grateful."

"It was financial." She held her chin defiantly high. "I came to Owanda so I could pay my bills and buy what I needed to buy."

He directed his gaze toward the miniature pine tree near the rink's entrance. The Christmas tree sat in a galvanized metal bucket, adorned with gold painted acorns. The branches hung heavy with whimsical miniature ice skates. So simple and perfect.

His expression softened. "How do you spend Christmas in California?"

"I tried to create an old-fashioned Christmas despite the seventy-five-degree weather. Several years ago, Lucy insisted we purchase a pre-lit upside-down Christmas tree, and I've used it every December. Lately, she's usually absent with whoever her current boyfriend happens to be, so Amelie and I attend Christmas Eve service at a local mission church."

"Sounds lovely," he said.

It was also lonely, but she wouldn't tell him that part.

"Christmas morning is spent baking sweet rolls and opening gifts, and in the afternoon we visit the local animal shelter," she said.

"No doubt looking for an animal with deformities you can rescue and take home."

She nodded. "Like Grumpy, our African grey. He's part of

the family, as Doc is now. Amelie knew I'd never be able to return that kitten after I took him home."

"I love animals almost as much as you do," he said.

She grinned. "Almost?"

"Animals create chaos."

"And they offer unconditional love and companionship."

"If rescue animals are your passion, then I support you." He kept her gaze. "Christmas Eve is a week away, and I'm hoping you and Amelie will spend it with me." His invitation was made softly, unbearable tenderness laced with guarded hope. "Lucy mentioned going to Las Vegas with Jacob for Christmas, and I don't want my two special girls to be alone. Michael doesn't have a large appetite, and I can't eat all my mother's turkey and chestnut stuffing by myself."

She smiled. "We both know you probably could eat all the turkey and a plateful of Christmas cookies besides. Lucy and I would love to have your metabolism."

She touched a light hand to his sleeve, and he moved closer, apparently pleased and surprised at her involuntary touch. She could almost sniff the sauerkraut and apples braised in white wine wafting from the Brandts' kitchen on Christmas Eve. When she was young, Christmas in her mobile home had smelled of cheap beer and musty odors. Her parents never seemed to realize it was Christmas.

"I'll let you know," she said.

His sigh was quiet, as if he were reconciled to the fact she might refuse. "Amelie would love my mother's cinnamon star cookies, and I kept my copy of *The Night before Christmas.*"

She swallowed the aching lump in her throat at the remembrance of him reading the book aloud, along with good-natured pantomime and laughter. "You're the most persistent man I've ever met."

"Although the book's a tad worn, it's our Christmas tradition to read it in its entirety."

"The book is only thirty-two pages long," she said wryly.

He tilted his head and laughed. "Is that a 'yes'?"

His laughter was infectious. She grinned. "Yes, and thank you. Amelie and I will love a real family Christmas celebration, and I enjoy seeing your mother and brother. They're such fun to be around."

The silence in the ice arena was comfortable, punctuated by the laughter of children and parents filing in for hockey practice. Comfort and contentment, emotions she hadn't felt in a long time.

"Did you know your smile warms this entire rink?" He took her hands in his and kissed her forehead and eyes, then brushed an affectionate trail to her lips. Their breaths mingled.

She darted a glance toward the entrance. "Not here."

His arms wrapped around her, and warmth flooded her veins. "We used to sit in this corner and kiss after hockey practice."

The look in his eyes was all male, and her pulse thumped a steady beat. "You were all sweaty."

He laughed, his lips close to hers. "I always searched the stands for you. I would've been crushed if you ever missed a practice or a game. Our team would've lost."

"And I was always cheering when you scored the winning goal."

His mouth pressed against hers with hurried urgency. She kissed him back, glorying in his need and the dizzying passion she'd always felt in his arms. He'd always chased away the aching sadness and isolation plaguing her.

A group of young boys with ice skates over their shoulders hooted as they passed. She pulled away, disoriented, incensed at herself and Fernando. They were at the public ice skating rink, kissing with the passion and abandon of two starry-eyed teenagers.

He gazed down at her with exquisite tenderness. "I can't believe we have a daughter."

"It wasn't right, what I did," she whispered. "It was selfish and self-centered to keep her from you. I'm so sorry."

"Thank you for apologizing. It means a lot." He stroked her hair. "You have the strength and resilience of a thousand men, and you're the most compassionate woman I've ever known. You'd never intentionally hurt anyone." He rested his chin against her forehead and whispered, "You know I've always loved you."

His gentleness prompted unexpected tears, and she ducked her head against his jacket. After all she'd done, he forgave her and he loved her.

"I kept telling Lucy I wanted to call you, but there was always another audition, another—"

"Shh. I understand. You don't need to explain further." His finger touched her lips. His gaze smoldered with admiration. The unique connection they'd felt since high school, that they were best friends and could confide everything to each other with no fear of being judged, surged between them. He bent his head to kiss her again, and she met him in the middle, finding confirmation of his forgiveness in one more kiss.

With a loud squeal of delight, Amelie, with a ring of whipped cream around her mouth, ran over to their booth, prompting a return to reason.

Margaret attempted to draw away, but Fernando draped his arm protectively around her shoulders. "On Christmas Eve, we'll attend services at the church, then have dinner at seven o'clock."

"Perfect." She couldn't help but note his expression of joy. Despite all the happiness she'd taken from him, she thought, with heartbreaking contrition, that he was looking toward the future.

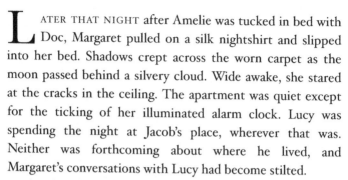

ATER THAT NIGHT after Amelie was tucked in bed with Doc, Margaret pulled on a silk nightshirt and slipped into her bed. Shadows crept across the worn carpet as the moon passed behind a silvery cloud. Wide awake, she stared at the cracks in the ceiling. The apartment was quiet except for the ticking of her illuminated alarm clock. Lucy was spending the night at Jacob's place, wherever that was. Neither was forthcoming about where he lived, and Margaret's conversations with Lucy had become stilted.

Amelie, though, was thrilled about her new-found daddy. Already she had blossomed under Fernando's watchful eyes, and her pale pallor had been replaced with a healthy glow. He'd proven in a short while he was indeed a wonderful father, and his mother had welcomed Margaret and Amelie with tears of delight. No recriminations, no turning away with aversion and loathing. She'd understood Margaret's sincere explanations and treated her like a daughter, just as she always had. Michael had demonstrated his magic tricks and chuckled when Amelie called him Uncle Michael. He'd also complained to Margaret that Fernando was preventing him from renting his own apartment.

"It's for your own good," Fernando had said. "Suppose you have another seizure and you're alone? I want to keep you safe."

Typical Fernando, Margaret had thought, always practical, always trying to protect everyone.

She sighed and tucked her hands behind her head. Wasn't this where they belonged—in her hometown, where she and her daughter could be loved? She enjoyed Fernando's company and valued his friendship. He made her laugh. He was trustworthy and neat and honest to a fault, and he supported her love of animals. Perhaps, she considered with a smile, they'd continue growing their family and be blessed with another child. Amelie didn't carry the sickle cell trait or syndrome, and neither did Margaret. They'd both been tested, and Fernando had responded to her news with a strangled cry of relief.

She rolled to her stomach and buried her head in her pillow. New York City was a few hours from Owanda by train. She'd check with her agent, and perhaps there were jobs on the East Coast better suited to her modeling career. If she had another child, there were categories for lifestyle models that she could age into while they raised a family. She smiled and imagined Fernando's delight when she told him, knowing in her heart he'd support her decision to continue modeling. She had reconciled herself to the fact she'd never be a movie star. So they'd never be wealthy, but she'd be able to keep her financial independence and work.

She gave up trying to sleep. Propping up the pillows, she watched the sleet clinking against her bedroom window, the snow outside white and frozen.

How did Fernando earn a living? He'd offered a vague explanation that his real estate office was on the other end of town, and he had a business in Florida. Judging by his expensive clothes and car, he must be selling a lot of homes.

Her smile deepened. He loved her. She'd seen it in his eyes, in his smile, and she loved him. And this time when he discussed marriage, she'd actively participate in the planning. Amelie would be the flower girl, strewing delicate red rose petals, and Pachelbel's Canon in D would swell from the church organ as Margaret walked down the aisle. With a sense of peace, she rested her head against the pillows and welcomed slumber, although her mind was busy and the ideas ran together. She was adding a scalloped hemline to the flared sleeveless wedding gown, as well as a crimson chiffon bow at the waist, when she slid beneath the covers and fell asleep.

This time, nothing would stop her fairy tale wedding to the man who had once been her prince.

CHAPTER THIRTEEN

"I've never attended a foreclosure auction." Lucy tightened the faux leopard fur belt around her waist and adjusted her periwinkle satin blouse to show more cleavage. "Am I overdressed?"

"Not if you plan on attending a mid-morning cocktail party," Margaret replied. She'd worn a proper cream silk blouse over a white camisole, a tan pencil skirt, and beige heels. On a whim, she'd added a jaunty red headband to offset her black wavy hair and add a festive air to her outfit.

"Jacob's taking me out to dinner. Does that count?" Lucy asked, her voice rising.

Jacob was a subject Margaret avoided. She'd come to an understanding with Lucy. As long as he wasn't mentioned, they wouldn't argue.

When Margaret didn't answer, Lucy rolled her eyes. "You shouldn't blame him for what happened. I'm the one who told him he could come to our apartment. I am, after all, a grown woman who can make her own decisions. Besides, Fernando forgave you, and you should forgive also."

"I understand. You're in love." *Again.* But Margaret didn't say that aloud.

She gazed at the ornate real estate office, a restored bank lobby. Marble floors and gleaming wood paneling were offset with tasteful crown molding.

Lucy's gaze followed Margaret's. "Real estate and property must be better than I imagined because someone's getting rich in this town. Who owns this building?"

Margaret shrugged. "I don't know much about real estate, but it's obvious some big company put a lot of thought into this restoration. I heard they're building apartments in this complex also."

Lucy adjusted the flashing poinsettia brooch on her collar.

Margaret covered her mouth with her hand to suppress a giggle. "Should you still be flashing?"

"Oops! The battery has a mind of its own." Lucy yanked at the chain, and the poinsettia returned to its red shiny state. "I hope none of these important people saw me flashing."

Margaret laughed aloud. "With any luck, they won't be interested in my dilapidated mobile home." She inspected a sign in the lobby listing the foreclosure properties, then nodded toward the glass elevator across the hall. "The auction is on the fourth floor." She opened her handbag and fingered the certified check for five thousand dollars. Her fingers were cold and clammy, and a premonition of disaster followed her. So much money—and the last of her savings. All those weeks of nonstop work at the mall, calming frustrated parents and crying toddlers, hadn't brought in as much money as she'd anticipated. Gus hadn't been able to work for several days because he'd developed a heart arrhythmia and she couldn't find a replacement Santa. The week before Christmas was one of the busiest times, and she'd been forced to shut down the Christmas display.

"Perhaps I should drop this entire auction idea and save money for more important things," she murmured.

"Now you're having second thoughts? All you've talked about for two months is buying back your trailer."

"I'm inexperienced in real estate. I've never attended a live auction."

"Don't take offense, but you're interested in something no one else wants. They'll probably give it to you."

She couldn't help but grin because Lucy was always brutally honest.

"Maybe it'll only sell for one thousand dollars and I'll have four thousand dollars left over."

Another call to her agent had gone unanswered, although she'd left a message requesting him to send her head shots and résumé to an affiliate agency in New York City. He at least had returned her call, just that morning, when she'd been in the shower. He'd left a voice mail regarding a feature film. He said it was urgent and to call him immediately, but everything in Hollywood was urgent. She would call him after the auction.

She smiled. Yes, things were definitely looking up, and Amelie would have a wonderful Christmas. With the money she hoped to save on the auction, she'd buy Amelie the doll-house, complete with furniture, tiny dishes and family pets, that she'd been eyeing in the mall.

As they stepped into the elevator, Lucy asked where Fernando had been lately.

"He had a lot of business to catch up on." Although when she'd pressed him for details, he'd been elusive. She had hoped they'd spend some time alone so she could tell him of her plans to settle in Owanda permanently, but she hadn't had the opportunity. He had called every night to talk with her and Amelie, but she wanted to tell him her decision in person. Now with Christmas Eve only a couple of days away, she'd surprise him then.

"When are you flying back to California?" Lucy asked.

Margaret shrugged, suppressing a secret smile. "I'm not sure."

"Jacob and I are flying to Las Vegas on Christmas Eve, then to California for New Year's. We'll rent an apartment once we get settled, so I won't be moving back in with you and Amelie."

Margaret nodded, and they rode the elevator in silence. When the door opened on the fourth floor, Fernando stood directly in front of them carrying a black leather briefcase. She heard his sharp intake of breath as he stepped back.

"Margaret?" He stared at her with a blank expression. She'd never seen him like this. His face was usually a road map showing every emotion.

Her eyes widened, and she sucked in a breath. She must've stepped from the elevator because the doors closed behind her with a ping. She felt her face flush. "Fernando?"

"What are *you* doing here?" Lucy blurted.

He gave a pained look and gripped his briefcase. "Just once, can you greet me with a simple hello?"

"What *are* you doing here?" Margaret asked.

His muscles bunched, causing his superbly tailored gray suit to crease at the shoulders. "There's a foreclosure property ... I'm interested in. What about you?" He spun to walk with them. He didn't brush a light kiss on her forehead as he usually did, nor did he touch her arm to guide her.

"My mobile home is in foreclosure and I'm buying it back," she said.

His dark brows set together in a frown. "Why would you want to do that?"

"Because it's mine."

"Not anymore. The bank owns it."

Lucy flashed an encouraging smile at Margaret. "Well, if Fernando's advising you, then you don't need me. I'll wait in the lobby and call Jacob, or maybe I'll get a tattoo on my left thigh." She waved a hand dismissively and clicked on her poinsettia pin. "Just kidding." She swiveled on her calfskin-leather stilettos and clicked down the hallway.

Margaret double-checked the room number, and Fernando followed her into a large area set up with armless chairs. She picked up a list of the auctions from a table at the entrance, then seated herself in the front row. He slid into the chair beside her and set his briefcase on his lap.

"You don't want your old trailer. It's a sad remembrance of those lonely years, and it's been empty so long it'll need numerous repairs," he said.

His flat dismissal of what she wanted and didn't want sounded a little too authoritarian. Her chin came up. "How would you know about the condition?"

"I'm in real estate, and trailers depreciate."

Her fingers tightened around the list. "I'm not buying it to make money." She swallowed. "It means a lot to me."

"You'll need to tear it down."

"That's exactly what I intend to do. I'm putting a house on the land."

Briefly, he closed his eyes. "Margaret." He touched her hand, the first time he'd touched her. "There's something you should know. I'm also bidding on the property."

She dropped the list onto the floor and was silent. When she bent to retrieve it, she could feel her whole body stiffen. "Why?" Her tone sounded pinched, like she couldn't get enough air in her lungs, or like a glass of cold water had been pitched at her face. That feeling of disaster hung in the air.

She took a deep breath and retrieved the list. Perhaps he was planning to gift it to her and Amelie as a Christmas surprise.

She looked at the list and saw that the starting bid for the trailer was one thousand dollars and thankfully affordable. However, the adjacent mobile home park, added to her listing, brought the price up to one hundred thousand dollars.

One hundred thousand dollars.

She pointed to the list. "Is there a mistake?"

"No, your trailer and the park are being sold as one parcel."

She raised her brows. "Why? My trailer was never in the mobile home park."

"Because I—"

He jerked around as a breathtakingly beautiful woman in a flowing variegated silk dress sashayed in, commanding the attention of the entire room. Heads swiveled as the woman headed straight for him.

"Surprise, darling." She pressed a kiss on his cheek while rubbing her hand on his forearm. "I love dove-gray suits on you."

His hands tensed into fists on top of his briefcase. "Diana, what are you doing here?"

She patted her shiny blonde hair, elegantly coifed and sprayed into place. "Dad and I flew up from Miami. He's talking with one of the bankers for additional financing. I wanted to be here to support you." Her hand stopped stroking his arm as her crystal-blue gaze raked Margaret with complete distaste.

Margaret drew back. "I don't believe we were introduced," she said to nobody in particular.

Diana seated herself on Fernando's left and then leaned around him. "You're the little pauper who ran off to California to enjoy her fifteen minutes of fame flaunting her body in a swimsuit. Fernando told me all about you."

Margaret flinched and swallowed. 'I'm sorry, but I don't know who you are."

Diana ran an intimate hand along his. "Hasn't he mentioned me? He's my father's real estate partner and I'm his fiancée."

The silence of an abandoned cemetery settled over the large room. Margaret stared down at the foreclosure list in her hands, trying to focus on it, but her eyes were swimming with tears. All the while he'd accepted her apologies, kissing her, holding her, nodding sympathetically, he'd been engaged to another woman.

She pushed back her chair and threw the list on the floor. She wouldn't be able to bid because her throat was closing.

He grabbed her hand. For a moment, she curled her fingers around his for support. Then she remembered and pulled from his grasp.

"I didn't know you were interested in your trailer or I never would've listed the parcels together," he said.

"You arranged this?" she whispered.

Diana heard her and laughed. "You should thank him. Perhaps you can give him your portion for what a rusty trailer's worth—five dollars."

He swung around. "Enough, Diana. That trailer was Margaret's childhood home." He turned to Margaret. "Please. I'll do what I can to fix this."

She shook her head, a frantic, insistent *no* as the auctioneer took the podium and outlined the auction rules. She tried to stand, but Fernando grabbed her hand firmly. Tears of righteous anger sprang to her eyes as she looked around, trying to spot a way out. Several people in the room were parents from the mall, and they smiled and waved, obviously recognizing her as the former swimsuit model who'd been in the elf costume.

Somehow, she held her chin high, waved back, and faced front again. She was the aspiring actress, she told herself.

The bid for the parcel started at one hundred thousand

dollars, and the price kept rising, thousands of dollars for a trailer park the developers planned to tear down. Or rather, Fernando and his real estate company. Mutely, she calculated the minutes until the auction was over and she could crawl away, far from him and his precious Diana. Far from the frozen town of Owanda. Far from elves and dwarfs. She stared at the floor as Fernando seized the winning bid, over half a million dollars. But she was done. It was over. And she couldn't bear to stay in the room another minute. She crumpled the list, tossed it in her purse, and pushed back her armless chair.

Fernando grabbed her hand again and he spoke quietly. "I'll talk with the auctioneer. Don't leave."

She shook off his hand and stood. "Lucy's waiting, and then I'm picking up Amelie after school."

"I'll call you tonight."

"Don't bother." She choked out the words. "Congratulations. You won."

Carefully, she composed her features to a cool disinterest. Her shoulders straight, she grabbed her purse and kept her gaze fixed ahead as she marched from the room. She rode the elevator alone to the first floor and Lucy, surprise, surprise, wasn't there.

Margaret walked slowly to her car. Sleet assaulted her cheeks along with the tears, and she slipped several times on the icy sidewalk. The disappointment inside her ached, a constant reminder of how elusive happiness was.

She started her car and stared at the frozen windshield. Must it always sleet? Where was the snow in this infernal town? Not the wet slushy snow or the icy snow they'd had so far, but those fluffy white flakes that were supposed to coincide with the Christmas season?

As a child, she had loved to wake up and gaze out her bedroom window at the piles of feathery snow that had fallen during the night. Sledding on crisp, cold mornings meant afternoon lunches of toasted cheese sandwiches and tomato soup, followed by cups of hot chocolate topped with frothy whipped cream.

Ha! She brushed her bangs aside, tore off the red head-band, and flung it to the backseat. None of those events had occurred in the Snow household. Her imagination was conjuring remembrances of a childhood she'd only read about in books.

She swiped at her eyes and chewed her trembling lip.

All this heartache. She never should've come back, and she'd go mad if she stayed in town another day. She'd book a direct flight for her and Amelie back to California on Christmas Day; airfares would probably be cheaper because of the holiday. If they left early morning, they'd arrive by noon because of the three-hour time difference.

They'd spend Christmas like they always had, attending a quiet church service and then serving at a rescue kennel. Perhaps they'd adopt an animal with half an ear, or half a tail, a cat or a dog no one else wanted. And they'd take the animal home and save it from being put down.

"Because their spirits aren't broken," one of the workers at a shelter had once said.

And Amelie would have an enjoyable Christmas, minus the snow, of course, because snow didn't fall in California.

Margaret sniffled and caught one of her tears with her tongue. She kept her gaze glued to the windshield, but the wipers kept freezing up. She had to keep stopping to clean the windshield because the wipers were so thin, they were worthless.

CHAPTER FOURTEEN

"I'm headed to the kitchen for some fudge. I read somewhere there are no calories in Christmas sweets." Lucy stopped at the entrance to Margaret's bedroom and plopped one hand on her hip. "You're supposed to laugh and correct me. It's a joke."

"I smiled. Does that count?"

Lucy sighed and shook her head. "Fernando called again. He's taking Amelie to a Christmas play after they have dinner. He said he's grating some type of egg noodle batter and Amelie is helping him. Shouldn't you talk with him before you leave?"

"It's spaetzle. His mother used to make it all the time." Margaret placed her suitcase on the bed and opened it. "He's seeing his daughter and will be with her until we leave for California."

"But he wants to see you too, and I'm tired of relaying messages back and forth between you two."

"There's nothing further to say." Her shoulders hunched forward. Surely the knot wanting to take up permanent residence in her stomach would dissolve. "No one can blame him for moving on after all these years, but I'm not discussing Diana with him."

It was too painful. She'd imagined a happy ending after their make-out session in the ice arena. He'd imagined one also, but with another woman.

She choked on her own fury, done with foolish dreams and crushing hopes. She'd wept each night since the auction with nothing to show for it but bloodshot eyes and a dejected spirit.

"Do whatever you want, you always do." Lucy's voice was clipped as she continued to the kitchen. "But I think you're throwing away a good life with him."

Margaret's cell phone rang. She picked it up while folding her favorite cotton blouse and placing it in her suitcase. "Hello?"

"Margaret? It's Sid, your agent. Why haven't you returned my call?"

Good question. She shook her head. "I'm sorry. There's a lot going on here."

An impatient huff rang through the line. "You know the feature film you auditioned for?"

The audition she'd botched. "Yes?"

"The casting director has slated you for one of the minor characters. Lots of bathing suit stuff, but your looks are what you're known for."

She tightened her grip on the phone. Her heart leaped. "You mean I got a role after all? Are there a lot of lines?"

"That's the good part. You have to walk beneath a waterfall and say how good the water feels on your skin, or something like that. Because it's a major motion picture, your salary will be in the high six figures."

She squeezed her eyes shut. A huge amount of money would ensure she'd have the funds to provide for Amelie's education and health needs for a long time. But the good part, he'd said. What was the bad part?

"Then you can move to New York City like you mentioned in your voice mail," Sid went on. She thought she caught something in his voice, a faltering, but he never faltered.

"I've had a change of heart and am moving back to California as planned," she explained.

Sid didn't respond to that. "There's one more thing," he said, and then hesitated. "When you walk beneath the waterfall ... you'll be topless. It's a view of your back, so not full frontal exposure. I'm assuming you're good with that because nowadays, it's expected."

Silence. A slow, sick feeling added to the knot in her stomach. This was life in the Hollywood lane, the fast road to success. "You know how I feel about nudity, Sid. Let me think about it."

"You can't keep these guys waiting, and this role is a great opportunity. There's a thousand actresses in line behind you."

"I realize that and thank you. I'll call you the day after Christmas."

She clicked off her cell and studied her suitcase. It was too small for the sweaters she'd bought in Owanda. She'd donate them to a women's shelter in the morning.

Grumpy squawked from its cage in the living room. Walking out there, she grabbed an orange from the basket on the floor and fed him several small pieces. He stared at her with pale gray eyes.

Lucy was slouched on the living room couch, a plateful of homemade chocolate fudge perched in her lap. Her gaze was glued to the television and a cartoon version of *A Christmas Carol*. Doc was curled up beside her. Lucy had already moved all of her clothes and personal items from the apartment, but a designer suitcase stood in the foyer.

"I couldn't help but overhear," she said around a mouthful of chocolate. "That was Sid on the phone."

"Yes, he offered me a part in the feature film I auditioned for."

That news prompted Lucy to sit up, which caused a landslide of fudge to the carpet. "Congratulations! Jacob will be thrilled because you'll get to know some powerful people."

"I'll be sure to put in a good word for him," Margaret said.

Lucy picked up the fudge and popped another piece in her mouth. "The one-second rule," she explained. Chewing thoughtfully, she added, "Jacob and I leave tomorrow, Christmas Eve. It doesn't matter if we'll be traveling on a holiday as long as we're together."

"And Amelie and I leave on Christmas morning."

Lucy hesitated. "I hate the thought of you being alone on Christmas Eve."

Margaret shook her head. "It's like any other day, and Fernando's family will keep Amelie entertained. I'll finish packing, then head to the office. I've hardly spent any time there since the mall job started, and I need to clean out my desk." She sighed and looked around. "I never had time to get a small Christmas tree, and I denied Amelie Christmas memories."

Lucy laughed. "You set up the forlorn tree at the office, and Amelie is enjoying a wonderful holiday. Your Christmas display at the mall was festive, she went ice skating, and she's spending time with her father. The Brandts always knew how to celebrate Christmas with lots of merriment and festivity."

Margaret swallowed. To change the subject, she asked, "How's Gus?"

"He was admitted to the hospital because of the arrhythmia, and the doctors had to insert a pacemaker. But everything's well now."

Margaret sighed. "I'll call him before we leave. He's been so good to Amelie."

A car horn beeped, and Lucy jumped from the couch. "Jacob's a great guy, but he can't keep track of time. He's an hour late, as usual." She gave Margaret a quick peck on the cheek and grabbed her coat and boots while cramming the last piece of fudge in her purse. "Merry Christmas! See you in California!"

Margaret turned off the television, instantly regretting the silence.

She sat on the couch to snuggle Doc, but the kitten permitted her one stroke before arching to be put down. "You'll be flying as carry-on baggage, so you better behave."

Animals were so much better than humans. They never broke your heart, never talked back. They simply wanted to love and be loved. If only humans could give love as freely.

Grumpy swung upside down in his cage and stared at her.

"We're going back to California," she said to the parrot. "You'll be flying as checked baggage."

No answer. She walked to his cage and began peeling an orange. She offered him a slice.

"If only you weren't deaf and could talk to me," she said.

The bird stopping swinging. "Change of heart," the parrot said.

She dropped the orange to the floor. "All this time, you could talk and were listening to us? We would've adopted you from the rescue shelter, no matter if you were deaf or not." She reached her hand into the cage and patted his head. "You were too cute to ignore."

Grumpy stood on his perch and wiped his beak. "Merry Christmas, spaetzle."

CHAPTER FIFTEEN

As Fernando strode toward the hospital entrance, he glanced at his watch, mentally planning every detail as Christmas Eve neared. First, he'd stop by his real estate office and finalize the mobile park sale. Then he'd head home to Amelie and his family to assist with last-minute Christmas Eve preparations. He tightened his grip on his briefcase, relieved he'd gotten one more gift for Amelie before the mall closed for the holiday. The air was brisk and cold, the smell of snow in the air, perfect for Christmas.

He pushed open the door to the hospital, mildly surprised to see Gus sitting in a wheelchair, a plump, beardless man with a twinkle in his sharp blue eyes.

"Ho, ho, ho," Gus said in his jovial Santa imitation. "I heard you were leaving for Florida. Don't take offense, but you look like you haven't slept in days."

Fernando scraped a hand over his jaw. He'd spent two sleepless nights staring at the ceiling in the dark, thinking about Margaret. She had smiled with such happiness as she'd admitted that she and Amelie would love a real family Christmas celebration with him.

"What are you doing at the hospital on Christmas Eve day?" Gus asked.

Fernando slid onto a bench near the older man. "I picked up my brother's doctor's report. He's recuperated nicely since the operation, and thankfully there's no more dialysis for him. His blood tests confirmed that the transplanted kidney is functioning properly. He'll take medication to prevent transplant rejection, but he's able to lead a normal life. And in turn, we're blessed to have him in our lives." Fernando cleared his throat, reminding himself not to take anything or anyone for granted. "Are you being discharged?"

"Yep. Waiting for my daughter to pick me up because our car is in the parking lot. The doctor was concerned about my heart and inserted a pacemaker. I'd like to think I can slide down the chimney with a sack of toys." Gus sighed. "But I'm feeling more tired than usual these days."

"Perhaps it's time you retired," Fernando said.

In the hospital archway, an animated display of old man winter, complete with snowflakes, began flashing and playing a cheerful Christmas tune.

"I'm supposed to quit drinking brandy and every other beverage I enjoy to avoid any heart complications, and the doctor wants me to sit around all day and do nothing," Gus said.

"Will you take his advice?"

"Maybe, as long as I can still play cards with someone." Gus shrugged, reached in his pocket, and tossed Fernando a crushed white beard. "Your brother can play Santa Claus next year."

Gus's hand had developed a small tremor. Illness was a funny thing because it made you appreciate life. How easy it was to become unappreciative of the things that really mattered. Fernando's mind flashed to his brother, and he knew that Michael would agree to the Santa role. He loved children and would probably add a magic trick or two. He placed the beard in his briefcase. "I'll mention it," he said.

"Margaret called me this morning. She and Amelie are flying to California tomorrow. Hardly any snow has fallen since they arrived." Gus glanced at the icy slush outside, apparently to prove his point.

Fernando stared at the revolving hospital door, not wanting to face the bitter defeat of losing her a second time. "Yes, Lucy told me. Amelie's creating a gingerbread house with my mother and brother this afternoon, and I'll take her back to their apartment early Christmas morning."

He didn't know how long he could bear that sort of living arrangement, with his daughter and Margaret three thousand miles away from him. What was she thinking by refusing to speak with him? She wouldn't give him an opportunity to explain. Didn't she understand he'd waited years before beginning a new life, settling for a wealthy woman who was happy to fund his work pursuits? *Settling.* What an interesting description of his relationship with Diana, but money had blinded him. Perhaps he'd wanted to prove to Margaret that he could be as successful as she had become.

"Can you imagine?" Gus asked. "Our little Margaret's been offered a role in a major motion picture. She'll be appearing on the big screen in all the movie theaters across the country."

Fernando's cell phone buzzed. He glanced at it; Diana's phone number was displayed on the screen. They had argued after the auction, and she'd left in a huff for Miami, leaving him an ultimatum that he better immediately follow her. He hadn't. He stared again at the revolving hospital door. Some of the people entering and leaving appeared to be patients; others were probably visiting family and friends. Young people walked quickly while older people shuffled along, some with canes.

"I'm planning an equitable arrangement and won't fight for custody." He scowled while he spoke, his expression contrary to his words. In reality, Margaret had responded to his phone calls with silence, as if they were opponents rather than former best friends, lovers, and parents to a beautiful five-year-old girl.

"So you'll be flying to California from time to time?"

"I don't fly. I'll take the train or bus," Fernando admitted.

"I was certain you two were meant for each other, but I must've been wrong. Diana, from what I've heard, is more your type."

Fernando fixed his gaze on a pole-mounted display of spiral snowflakes near the hospital entrance. "Diana's goals aren't complicated and she leaves the business decisions to me."

"And Margaret would fight you all the way."

Fernando chuckled. "Yes, she probably would."

"It's a shame, letting a woman with her kindness and bravery slip through your fingers a second time. She's got such a big heart." Gus nodded slightly. "But I understand Diana's father's wealth is enticing to an enterprising man like you."

This time, Fernando met Gus's gaze head-on. "I don't need her father's money."

Gus stayed quiet for so long that Fernando continued to stare at him.

"Once you tear down the mobile home park and Margaret's old trailer, how will you fund an outlet mall that'll cost millions of dollars?" Gus finally asked.

Fernando shook his head. "I've shelved the idea for an outlet mall. Instead, I'm turning the area into a park with a man-made pond for fishing in the summer and ice skating during the winter months, something the entire community can enjoy at no cost. And I'm developing some other plans also."

"Margaret wanted to build a new home on her old property. She mentioned a white bungalow with a red front door." Gus performed a brilliant interpretation of a man who'd just said something he shouldn't by putting a hand over his lips.

"Sounds like you're describing my childhood home." Fernando's heart did a quick flutter. Could she have been yearning for his house all these years?

"Margaret said you're leaving early Christmas morning for Miami," Gus went on. "She's spending this afternoon at her office cleaning out her desk."

Fernando tightened his grip on his briefcase. "Good to know." All this cheerful information about Margaret was wearing thin on his taut nerves. And where was Gus's daughter? It didn't take that long to retrieve a parked car.

"What has Margaret told you about the Hollywood film?" Gus asked.

"We haven't spoken, remember?" he said impatiently.

"They want her to wear a bathing suit for the role. Or rather, half a bathing suit."

Fernando rose to his feet. "Is that what she said?" His gaze narrowed as he frowned. It might be Christmas, the time of harmony and good cheer, but he was in the mood for a confrontation. She damn well wouldn't be appearing topless in any film.

Gus's mouth was wreathed in a wide grin as Fernando turned on his heel without saying good-bye and strode away with long, purposeful strides.

"Merry Christmas!" Gus called. "There's snow in the forecast. Drive slow."

∾

A S HE DROVE to Margaret's office, Fernando phoned his mother to tell her he'd be later than planned. "Start preparing the turkey without me," he said. "And tell Amelie I'll be back soon."

He kept seeing the image of Margaret in that tiny iridescent yellow bikini plastered on the cover of a sports magazine a couple of years ago. Hadn't he stood by as other men gazed lustfully at her enticing body, all the while making lewd comments? That had been a difficult and trying time in his life, and he had decided once and for all that she didn't want him. And then he'd heard she had returned. He'd gone to her office to tell her about the auction, at the last minute taking the gift he'd bought her years before. He'd kept it in his bureau all these years. Upon seeing her, he quickly realized he still loved her with an urgency he couldn't explain. But if he was honest with himself, he'd known that all along.

He sighed inwardly. If she hadn't left him without a word after graduation, if her hair wasn't the perfect shade of ebony, if she wasn't so proud and determined, he'd never have gotten engaged to Diana in the first place.

He stopped the car and punched in Diana's number, doing what he should've done months ago.

CHAPTER SIXTEEN

E very few minutes Margaret pulled her white Volvo over to the side of the road, got out and scraped the snow off the windshield. Her cold car engine idled loudly. The warning of an impending snowstorm—which seemed to have arrived already — blasted from the radio, and she hoped to be finished packing things from her office by dusk. One could usually count on a snowy Christmas in Owanda, which brought with it, she realized with surprise, not a sense of frustration but of tranquility.

She'd never excelled at parallel parking but found a space near her office. The streets were noticeably quiet, the stillness broken only by ice crackling beneath her boots as she walked. Nonetheless, she could feel an air of anticipation for the special holiday. She sniffed appreciatively the scent of wood fireplaces and wondered how she and Amelie could ever leave the town that was her home.

She fumbled with her office entry keys and then flicked on the lights in the cold hallway as she entered. The worn waiting room chairs sat empty. Glossy magazines featuring movie stars and their secret lives were displayed neatly on the coffee table. She picked up one of the magazines. People believed movie stars were blessed with physical attractiveness and a charisma that hurled them into stardom. She'd learned it was also hard work and required difficult decisions. In a society valuing wealth and fame, she'd succeeded. All she'd had to give in return was her integrity.

She placed the magazine back on the table. One more set of keys and she entered her office. She loosened her coat, wet from the snow, and slung it over a chair. Then she wandered aimlessly around the stark, quiet room.

She pulled a chair up to the window and watched snowflakes falling thickly on the streetlights. Cheery red bells and silver holiday trimmings were being covered by a feathery white blanket. A true winter wonderland icing everything in its path.

Now, with no one around, she could congratulate herself on all she'd achieved and grieve for what she'd subsequently lost. Fleeting success, brief wealth, an opportunity to pursue her greatest dream—a film career.

Check. Check. Check.

She brushed tears from her cheeks. But, oh, what she'd sacrificed. She'd defied Fernando, shamed him, lied to him, while believing that, somehow, he'd always wait for her. A bleak pain grew in her throat because she'd lost a man who'd truly loved her. In return for his trust and affection, she'd caused him to be an object of ridicule in his beloved home-town and kept his daughter from him. She wanted to replay Diana's intimate voice while she'd touched his arm posses-sively at the auction, the insults she'd hurled at Margaret, and her stunning beauty.

Instead, Margaret remembered the way Fernando had held her protectively in his arms at the public ice skating rink, how he'd teased her about her deaf parrot the first day in her office, or when he'd whispered in a voice tender with emotion, "I can't believe we have a daughter."

She stared out the window at the never-ending snow, the pearly-gray clouds covering the sky. If she didn't hurry, she'd be stranded in her office on Christmas Eve. Quickly, she walked to her desk and knelt on the floor. A pile of boxes sat beside her, which she loaded with pens, pencils, and blank applications. Fortunately, she'd never unpacked several boxes that still stood in a haphazard pile against the wall.

She opened the top drawer of her desk and hesitated. His beautifully wrapped gift sat unopened. She took it out and turned it around with her fingers. At the bottom was a small card. With a choked sigh she read his bold handwritten script aloud: "To my snow white princess, all my love."

She drew a long tortured breath and slowly expelled it. Although she hadn't spent any time at her office, she should've opened the gift when he'd first offered it to her.

Hesitating, she stood and set the gift on her desk. Too late now. She'd take it back to California and open it there, a token gift for herself on Christmas Day.

Somehow, she had to accept his impending marriage to another woman, a sophisticated woman who made Margaret feel unrefined and gauche. She leaned against her desk and briefly closed her eyes. How could she live in California and raise their daughter without him?

She straightened away from her desk. What was she doing? She'd declared to anyone who asked that she made her own decisions and therefore controlled her own destiny. She would create a new life in Owanda, and Amelie could continue to see her father and his family. Sure, it would be difficult knowing he was with Diana, but he'd never be so unkind as to flaunt their happiness and break her heart. Besides, her heart was already broken.

She reached for her cell phone. This time she would truly

be the woman she wanted to be, a woman her daughter could be proud to call *Mommy*.

Your agent will never speak to you again if you make this call, a little voice in her mind rebuked. You're giving up everything you worked so hard for. Hollywood is an unforgiving town and won't forget.

Quickly she dialed Sid's number before she changed her mind.

Her call immediately went to voice mail. "The answer is no, Sid," was all she said. She pressed the end button on the phone. Somehow she knew that Hollywood would roll on without her. In the space of a brief phone call, she'd lost her Hollywood identity so she could establish a new one by creating a permanent home for her and her daughter.

The front office door slammed and footsteps strode purposefully through the hallway. Her office door flew open as he barged in, a familiar, handsome man from upstate New York in a well-tailored navy suit. He said nothing, just wheeled a suitcase into the middle of the room with one hand. In the other he held out a package wrapped in gold foil paper and tied with silver ribbon. His chocolate-brown eyes stared into hers.

You know I've always loved you, he'd whispered to her in the ice arena.

"I have a gift," he said aloud.

The room tilted, and she lurched from her chair. She nodded and swallowed, hoping to control her trembling voice. "You offered me a gift wrapped exactly like that six weeks ago." She pointed to the neatly wrapped package on her desk. "So now I have two."

He placed it beside its identical twin on her desk. "This one isn't for you."

She drew back to admire both gifts, then stared down at her hands.

To do something, anything, not to meet his probing gaze, she turned her gaze to the small Christmas tree on the corner of her desk. A sad reminder of how little she'd put into holiday decorating, its spindly branches were bare.

"Poor forlorn little thing," she whispered.

He leaned closer. His nearness was disconcerting, a hairs-breadth away. "Anything I can do to help the situation?"

"Do you know anyone who can decorate a Christmas tree?"

He grinned boyishly and took a step nearer. "I load up a tree with lots of tinsel because that disguises any imperfections. Small, twinkling colored lights and a star at the top works wonders."

She smiled. "Twinkling lights? You sound like a television commercial."

"Your mind always seems to gravitate toward Hollywood."

In a small voice she said, "Not anymore."

He came around her desk, pulling his suitcase, and gazed silently at her.

She dug her nails into her palms. "Are you leaving for Florida this evening instead of tomorrow so you came here to say good-bye?" she asked. "If so, where's Amelie?"

"Our daughter's building a gingerbread house with my mother. And no, I'm not leaving for Florida, I'm flying to California." There was a curiously quiet gravity in his voice. "With you."

She blinked, brushing her bangs from her eyes, and then she stared at him.

"I don't understand. Amelie and I are staying in Owanda."

He dropped the handle of the suitcase to the floor. "You mean I won't have to fly to California and live there?"

"Not unless you're planning on becoming an actor."

His eyes held a sheen of tears. "That settles it then."

"Settles what?"

"Where we're going to live in order to be together." He closed the space between them and pulled her to him, wrapping his arms around her. "I've missed you so much."

He smothered her joyous murmur with his kiss. "Not as much as I've missed you," she was finally able to say.

His breathing was ragged when he lifted his head. "Will you marry me?"

"As long as you're not marrying anyone else." She tilted her head back and looked up into his earnest gaze.

"No one but you, my princess." With a brief nod, he added, "Diana wasn't in the best of humor when I called off our engagement, but she'll find another man before the New Year rings in." He pressed her head against his chest. "What about your movie role?"

"I'm not an actress, I'm a mother."

"And soon to be my wife," he added.

This was where she belonged. The exquisite feeling of his strong lean body fitting against hers and his hands massaging her back made her shudder, fearing that if they ever broke contact, her life would be shrouded under a vast emptiness she couldn't bear.

He tangled his hands through her hair. "Have I ever mentioned you remind me of Snow White?"

"About a thousand times. It's embarrassing to be named for a fairy-tale woman who was tricked into eating a poison apple by a witch."

"But first she lived with dwarfs who took care of her."

She gazed straight into his deep chocolate gaze. "I can't imagine living with seven men when one will do perfectly."

"I love you," he whispered solemnly. "I've always loved you."

She choked back tears of joy. "And I've always loved you."

He sat on her chair and settled her onto his lap. He

clasped her tighter as she laid a hand on his unshaven jaw. "Merry Christmas, darling," she said.

His eyes took on a devilish gleam. "It's not often we're alone, between deaf parrots and one-eyed kittens and our daughter." He took her lips in one long kiss and then eyed the pile of boxes on the floor. Slowly he unbuttoned the top button of her cardigan sweater and gathered her body close to his. "I have a plan. If I placed those boxes straight across on the floor as a bed ..."

～

TWO PAIRS of footsteps ran through the hallway.

"Mommy! Daddy! Look what I got!" Amelie's loud voice echoed through the room as she placed a tiny calico kitten with no tail on the desk between the two gifts wrapped in gold paper. She signed eagerly, "Uncle Michael said you'd be here because Daddy called him. We stopped at the animal shelter first."

Margaret leaped up from the pile of boxes and quickly buttoned her sweater. She crossed the room to hug her daughter, then looked at Fernando who had quickly stood as well. "You arranged this? You knew they were coming?"

He glanced at his watch and then glared at his brother striding quickly into the office. "You're a half hour early."

Michael tapped his hearing aid fitted unobtrusively behind his left ear. "Sorry, I didn't hear you."

"Michael, you're driving?" Margaret asked.

He nodded. "I bought a car, and I'll move into my new apartment at the end of the month. I got a good job with a prestigious real estate office located at the other end of town."

Margaret stared at the kitten attempting to scramble off

her desk. "Amelie, we can't possibly take on another rescue animal," she signed.

"Yes, we can, Mommy."

Fernando and Michael nodded simultaneously.

Margaret searched her mind for an explanation. With a helpless glance around the room, she asked and signed, "Can someone please tell me what everyone seems to know except me?"

Michael answered. "My twin brother isn't building an outlet mall on the mobile home property. He's building a public park for everyone to enjoy, and I'm in charge of the development."

"And, Mommy, where your house used to be, Daddy is building a brand new animal rescue shelter. It's a secret and a surprise."

Fernando strode to Margaret and Amelie and put his arms around them both. "It's a no-kill shelter." He spoke slowly and directly to Amelie so that she could lip-read. "We'll offer free spaying and neutering, as well as training people to provide good homes for these animals. But only on one condition."

Laughter and giggles from Michael and Amelie greeted his announcement. Margaret turned to face him. "We can only keep five animals at a time in our home?"

"Even better."

Margaret attempted to hide her smile. "And what is that condition?"

"That you'll work by my side as an equal partner."

"Got it all planned?"

He shrugged. "Call it a character flaw." He reached for the two gifts on her desk, handing one to her and the other to Amelie. "Will you please do me the honor of finally opening this?"

She laughed. "Only if Amelie opens hers too."

"You go first, Mommy," Amelie said.

"They're similar. You can open them together," Fernando prompted.

Amelie unwrapped her gift quickly and held up a tiny diamond necklace with a fine gold chain. "Daddy, I love it! Put it on me."

He fastened the necklace around her neck and she twirled in a proud circle.

He laughed. "Mommy's next," he said.

Margaret slowly unwrapped the gift, placing the gold foil on her desk. She snapped the lid up on a small box in the shape of an apple, exposing a small, exquisite single diamond. She stared at him. The laughter was gone, and his look had changed to solemn hopefulness. He seemed unsure, almost hesitant. "Do you like it?"

She gazed at him a long moment. "I love it."

"I bought this diamond for you a long time ago, after our graduation. It's small. I know it's small. I can get a bigger one if you want."

She shook her head, laughing through tears of happiness. "It's perfect."

"You can make it into a necklace, or a ring."

She held the diamond up to the light to admire it. "I prefer a ring."

He pulled her and Amelie closer to his chest. "I love you both so much."

"When's the wedding?" Michael asked. "I'll be the best man."

"Tomorrow," Fernando said.

Margaret shook her head. "Impossible. We'll need at least six weeks to plan the wedding. Besides, no church will marry us on Christmas Day."

"My church will. It's all planned," he said with a smile. "Assuming we're not snowed in."

Margaret twined her arms around him. "You mean you can't control the weather?"

He grinned. "Unfortunately, even I have limitations."

She narrowed her eyes. "Weren't you planning on flying to California with me? Did you have a wedding planned on both coasts?"

He offered an impish grin. "Lucy is on standby. The wedding would've been quickly arranged, and she even offered to skip Las Vegas and fly directly to California. Owanda was my first choice, though."

"I'll be the flower girl," Amelie signed. "A Christmas wedding, Mommy! We can have it outside in the snow, and Daddy can rent a sleigh, and then we can get a horse." She picked up the kitten. "Won't it be fun?"

Fernando wiped his eyes and held his daughter closer. "Amelie, I love you, sweetheart." He kissed her, then Margaret.

Amelie giggled and signed, "And we all lived happily ever after!"

The End

A NOTE FROM JOSIE

Dear Reader,

Thank you for reading *A SNOWY WHITE CHRISTMAS!* I hope you enjoyed my sweet romance. Please help other people find this book and post an online review.

I love going home for the holidays, and especially enjoy second chance romances. Margaret and Fernando were a joy to write.

Happy Reading!

Josie Riviera

This book is available in ebook, Audiobook, paperback, and large print paperback.

Spotify Play List Here.

Love sweet romance Christmas stories? Be sure to check out:

Sweet Peppermint Kisses

1-800-CHRISTMAS

A Portuguese Christmas

Aloha to Love

Candleglow and Mistletoe

A Christmas To Cherish (Inspirational)

A Snowy White Christmas

Holly's Gift (Inspirational)

A Chocolate-Box Christmas

and the boxed sets:

Holiday Hearts Volume 1

Holiday Hearts Volume 2

Holiday Hearts Book Bundle Volume 3

RECIPE FOR PEANUTTY CHOCO SURPRISES COOKIE

A favorite combination- chocolate and peanut butter!
Yields approximately 8 dozen cookies

Ingredients:

2 cups Peanut Butter (any brand- smooth or crunchy, and may use reduced fat, if desired.)

2 sticks butter (leave out of refrigerator at least 1-2 hours beforehand)

2 cups packed brown sugar

4 eggs

4 cups flour

2 tsp. baking powder

2 teaspoons cinnamon
1 bag candy kisses, wrappers removed

Cream peanut butter, butter, and sugar. Beat in eggs. Combine flour, baking powder, and cinnamon. Add gradually to peanut butter mixture until well blended. Stir by hand.

Chill dough at least 60 minutes for easier handling.

For each cookie, roll 1 teaspoon of dough into small ball and place on ungreased cookie sheet. Press in candy kiss. Bake for 10-12 minutes in 350 degree oven. After cooling, sift confectioners sugar on top, if desired.

ABOUT THE AUTHOR

USA TODAY bestselling author, Josie Riviera, writes Historical, Inspirational, and Sweet Romances. She lives in the Charlotte, NC, area with her wonderfully supportive husband. They share their home with an adorable shih tzu, who constantly needs grooming, and live in an old house forever needing renovations.

To receive my Newsletter and your free sweet romance novella ebook as a thank you gift, sign up HERE.

Become a member of my Read and Review VIP Facebook group for exclusive giveaways and FREE ARC's.

josieriviera.com/
josieriviera@aol.com

ACKNOWLEDGMENTS

An appreciative thank you to my patient husband, Dave, and our three wonderful children.

ALSO BY JOSIE RIVIERA

EXCERPT CHAPTER ONE: A PORTUGUESE CHRISTMAS

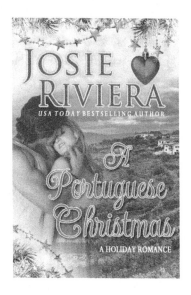

It was simply the way it was in Portugal, another morning dawning so brilliantly. Dappled sunbeams reflected off the Atlantic Ocean; the surf pounded along a long, sweeping beach.

So this was a Portuguese December, Krystal Walters

thought. It was so different from the cold weather battering her hometown of Newport, Rhode Island.

Here in Portugal, the sun never stopped shining.

She shaded her eyes, admiring the shimmering turquoise water. Feet snug in booties and reef socks, she wiggled her toes in the golden sand.

Hurray! Her anticipation grew with each breath of brisk, salty air. After a grueling year-long championship tour, the World Surf League ranked her as one of the top seventeen women surfers in the world. She actually stood on Medão Grande Beach's shoreline in Peniche, Portugal.

She tucked her waxed surfboard under her arm, hoisted her belongings, and headed for the competitor's area to check out the scheduled surf heats. Earlier that morning, she'd showered at the Oasis, an inexpensive hotel, and surfed for a short while. She'd encountered a sizeable wave and had spent a few seconds underwater. An hour had passed, and she still felt winded.

Shake it off.

Nothing would stop her, certainly not a little time underwater.

She gripped her water bottle, drained the contents, and refilled.

Slinging her lucky striped beach towel over her shoulder, she regarded the panoramic view of sky, tidal channels and mountains.

I wish you were here to see all this, Ernie.

A scream of sorrow slammed into her chest. Her carefree marriage to Ernie had lasted four months. And then, a week prior to their first Christmas together, he'd drowned while surfing.

"A huge wave will pack a big punch," the emergency medical responder had remarked. "Rip currents are drowning machines."

Ernie's death had left her disheartened. To escape a despair that never went away, she turned inward. Never again would she rely on anyone for emotional support. She couldn't bear the pain of loss, of abandonment, of defeat.

Sam Larson, an American surfer competing in the men's event, came to stand beside her. Playfully, he snatched her towel and dangled it in front of her. "Nervous?"

She seized her towel from him. "Absolutely."

"Ready to win?"

"I'm always out to achieve my personal best."

Sam nodded toward the voluptuous, sun-kissed brunette woman effortlessly riding a twelve-foot wave. "I gather from Wilhelmina's gutsy performance, she's aiming to win the preliminary competition too."

Krystal thoughtfully sipped from her water bottle. "She's an epic surfer."

"You're more proficient. Glad you're able to compete again. How long were you off the circuit?"

"Three years."

Sam's green-eyed gaze caught hers. The proverbial surfer dude, all bronzed skin and long, bleached-blond hair. "We missed you."

"Thanks." She swallowed the tightness in her throat and stowed the water bottle in her board bag. Affectionately, she patted her surfboard. "Angel and I are glad to be back."

"Angel?"

"My surfboard's name is Angel. You?"

"Umm, no. Although one of my buddies named his surfboard Rhino."

Krystal laughed. "I've always had a love affair with the ocean. I hope to generate a sponsorship from one of the swimsuit companies."

"Don't we all?" Sam smirked.

"Actually, lately, I've enjoyed sketching and designing swimsuits."

"Submit your designs. All the women's swimwear companies are represented here."

"Someday. For now, I'm here to surf."

Sam's smile was quick. "Conditions, swell models and the weather forecast are all textbook."

"Textbook is reassuring. I want to get out of Portugal as soon as possible."

"So you'll use all your feminine blonde, blue-eyed energy to accept your first-place winnings and leave this impressive climate behind?"

Krystal pulled sunblock from her purse and rubbed it on her nose and cheeks. "After the finals on December nineteenth, I'll return to Rhode Island."

"The purse is $15,000," Sam said.

"And if I win, I'm building an in-law apartment onto my bungalow so that my dad can live with me. We plan to celebrate Christmas together."

She was done with grief and heartache, and finally ready to celebrate the holidays again.

She scanned the spectators mobbing the shoreline, pleased to see her cousin Veronica, along with Veronica's husband, Clemente, and their twin six-year-old boys waving like mad cuckoo clocks in Krystal's direction. Veronica wore a wide-brimmed straw hat that covered her crimped auburn hair, a long rainbow-colored skirt, and pink floral scarf. Draped around her neck hung a camera and binoculars.

Krystal assumed her merriest smile and waved back. To cheer her on, they'd driven two hours from their olive farm in Évora. There was no reason for them to know her unease, or how much was at risk if she lost.

A tall man with thick, wavy black hair stood near Veronica. He crossed his tanned, muscular arms over his creased white shirt, and his worn denim jeans emphasized his fit physique. His expression was one of utter indifference to the entire competition—the crowd's lively applause, the announcer's incessant bullhorn, and the loud riffs of a guitarist strumming and singing that he wished all Portugal girls could be California girls.

Krystal studied the man's handsome features. No doubt he was Clemente's younger brother, Adolfo Silva. Although the men resembled each other, Clemente's softer, paler qualities suited his office environment, whereas Adolfo was tall and broad-shouldered, projecting an aloof strength.

Veronica had high praise for Adolfo. He worked the olive groves and consistently strove to build a more profitable farm.

How had Veronica persuaded her workaholic brother-in-law to attend a surfing competition? His stance was as rigid as a floorboard, a touch of arrogance in the set of his chiseled jaw. He glanced at his watch before bending to rescue one of the twin boys when the other hit him over the head with a beach ball. Adolfo muttered something and Veronica frowned, placing her freckled hands protectively on each boy's hair.

Under dark brows, Adolfo's gaze swept over Krystal, lingering on her form-fitting wetsuit.

Krystal felt her face heat. He was much too bold. Her wetsuit protected her body from the cold water. She wasn't a female specimen to be gawked at, as if she were wearing a skimpy bikini.

Haughtily, she met his stare.

His lips quirked.

Chin held high, she pivoted. She pegged him as one of those smooth-talking Mediterranean men who assumed any woman could be charmed by his lazy smile.

The announcer called her assigned heat.

She tucked the sunblock in her purse, secured the surf-board leash to her ankle and dismissed the fluttering in her stomach. Shaking out her hands, she tugged on her wetsuit gloves.

Sam clapped her shoulder. "See you on the nineteenth."

"Thanks. You'll surf great too." She snapped up her surf-board and quickened her pace to the water's edge.

An unexpected dizziness made her pause.

Ignore it.

She paddled into the cool waters while the head judge declared her wave priority. Krystal chose a large, walled wave that allowed her to gather plenty of speed, and she quickly reached the wave's velocity.

Within a second, she mounted her board and rode the twelve-foot crest. The sun on her face, the water around her, the natural movement of the ocean waves beneath her feet—this was her world.

The judges assessed swiftness, athletic power and flow. She was adept at a variety of difficult maneuvers and planned to perform them.

Yes, there were risks. And dangers. And consequences.

At the top of the wave, she stayed low and widened her stance to prepare for takeoff. She'd launch into the air, rotate and drop back down into the same wave. The key was to stay focused.

"Naive interference!" a man's voice from the milling spectators called out.

Her concentration broke for a beat. Another surfer took off on the inside of the wave directly in front of her. Krystal had the right of way, and this unexpected surfer was snaking.

She positioned to change direction, and a sudden steep wave barreled straight for her.

Losing control ... losing control of the board.

As she was sucked under, the water's force gripped her

body in an unforgiving embrace. Nearly exploding in her chest, her heartbeat raced.

"A huge wave will pack a big punch."

Stay calm. Don't panic.

She curled into a fetal position, her elbows shielding her face, bracing for the imminent body slam sure to follow.

*** End of Excerpt *A Portuguese Christmas* by Josie Riviera ***

Want more? Keep reading A Portuguese Christmas.

FREE on Kindle Unlimited!

Made in the USA
Columbia, SC
04 October 2020